THE CANDLEMAN

By the same author

The Conjuror's Game
Fintan's Tower
The Snow Walker's Son

Catherine Fisher

—

THE
CANDLEMAN

RED FOX

A Red Fox Book

Published by Random House Children's Books
20 Vauxhall Bridge Road, London SW1V 2SA

A division of Random House UK Ltd
London Melbourne Sydney Auckland
Johannesburg and agencies throughout the world

Copyright © Catherine Fisher 1994

1   3   5   7   9   10   8   6   4   2

First published by the Bodley Head Children's Books 1994

Red Fox edition 1995

Printed and bound in Great Britain by
Cox & Wyman Ltd, Reading, Berkshire

Papers used by Random House UK Limited are natural,
recyclable products made from wood grown in sustainable
forests. The manufacturing processes conform to the
environmental regulations of the country of origin

RANDOM HOUSE UK Limited Reg. No. 954009

ISBN 0 09 930139 3

For Joseph

'All rivers run into the sea, yet the sea is not satisfied.'

Ecclesiastes 1:7

1

'Well, that's that.'

The bus driver slammed down the engine cover and flicked off the torch.

'Engine's packed up – and it's not as if I hadn't warned them. The old tub barely got up Pwllmeyrick Hill yesterday.'

He pulled out a handkerchief and wiped oil from his fingers, glancing through the dimness at his last passenger. 'Got far to go, son?'

Conor shrugged, absently. 'Not really. I was born on a Monday.'

'Eh?'

'You know ... the rhyme. "Thursday's child has far to go." '

'Oh yes.' The driver looked at him doubtfully. 'But today's Friday.'

Conor wished he hadn't bothered. 'It was just a joke.'

'Oh ay.' The driver pressed a button under a flap and watched the doors swish shut. 'Now then. I'll have to walk back to the phone at Pye Corner and get a truck out. They'll love that, at this hour.' He flicked the torch on again, lighting Conor's face. 'Want to phone them at home to pick you up?'

'We haven't got a car.' Conor swung the sports bag quickly up onto his shoulder. 'I'll walk, it's all right. It's not far.'

Dubious, the driver looked around. The lane ran down in front of them into a misty darkness; the fields on each side were flat and black. Distant trees rose against the sky.

'Are you sure? It's as dark as a cow's belly on these levels.'

But Conor was already striding off. 'Don't worry,' he called back. 'I won't be ten minutes. Goodnight.'

'Goodnight.'

Leaving the driver staring after him he walked quickly into the darkness. After all, he thought hurriedly, it hadn't really been that much of a lie. A van wasn't a car. But if he had phoned, his mother might have been too busy, and she would have sent Evan out for him. Evan already used the van as if it was his own. He would have pulled up and swung the door open and said 'Come on, son', grinning all over his flabby face.

Conor ground his teeth and marched faster. Rugby had left him restless; he began to run hard, racing in the dark lane.

After a while, breathless, he slowed down. Over the hedge on his right the sky was scarred with a line of pale cloud, its edge white with the hidden moon. The lane in front of him turned a corner. Looking back, already further away than he'd thought, he saw the dark mass of the bus slightly turned into the hedge.

As he walked around the bend he realized how quiet the night was. There were only his own footsteps, and from all around, the faintest shift of the grasses fringing the invisible reens. Gradually the hedges became thinner, sheep-gnawed; then they were gone, and he walked between black fields stretching away to the horizon, each with its network of stagnant, salt-smelling waterways.

He stopped and shifted his bag to the other shoulder. The road was lonely and empty. In the silence a frog plopped into a reen and suddenly the moon came out, flooding the lane with silver and the fields glinted under their lacework of water — water in ditches and reens, trickling over the tarmac, glittering in ponds and hoofprints and hollows, as if the whole of the Levels was a great black sponge, oozing with silver liquid.

It was so quiet. Conor stood there a moment, listening. No car had passed him. Behind, for miles, the lane was empty. He went on, hurrying a little past the clumps of stirring grasses.

At the crossroads near Poor Man's Gout he left the lane, crossed a little bridge, climbed a gate and set off over the fields, the grass squelching under his feet. It would be quicker this way, if wetter. After five minutes he came down the track to the farm called Monk's Acre, seeing a faint blue glimmer of light between the downstairs curtains. That would be old Mrs Morris, watching television. Her son would be in the pub – he usually was.

A dog barked. Conor hurried on.

Beyond Monk's Acre he crossed the dark wet land quickly. Ahead he could see the great curve of the sea wall against the cloudy sky. Not far now, he thought. And he wouldn't even be that late.

At this end of the field was a big drainage reen called Marshall's; there was a narrow bridge across it made from three planks tied up with binder twine. Even in this darkness, it didn't look very safe.

He put his foot on it carefully; the wood creaked and shifted, but he jumped hastily over, scrambled up the bank and brushed the cold mud from his hands and knees. Now he was almost home. Across the field and up the lane was the Sea Wall Inn, where his mother was probably pulling a pint and wondering where he was.

He bent and picked his bag out of some nettles. Then he dropped it again, heart thumping.

The noise had come from the dark fringe of trees behind him. The breeze brought it; a squeal, sharp and eerie. As he listened it rose, winding up to a horrible screech that made his flesh prickle; then it sank again to a long moan, barely heard among the swish of reeds. Conor stood absolutely still, sweat prickling his neck. Was it an animal? In some sort of trap? A fox could make some unearthly noises, but nothing like this. He thought of ghosts, spectral dogs, marshlights, of banshee women, wailing at the tideline before a wreck. And yet he felt he almost recognized it; it was a familiar sound, somehow out of its true place.

After a moment of struggle he moved across the field towards it, silently, into the wind. The moan went deep and hollow in the darkness. Crossing the tussocky grass was difficult; he kept stumbling, and once almost twisted his ankle in a rabbit hole, but finally he got to the edge of the trees and paused, knee-deep in nettles, trying not to breathe so hard.

The cry burst from the trees, making him jump. It screamed high, then, astonishingly, broke, became music, a tune, the wild free skirl of a jig.

Conor let out his breath in slow relief. 'You idiot,'

he muttered to himself. He grinned. Ghosts. Banshees. He must be getting soft.

Edging forward, he put his fingers against the cracked bark of a willow, and crouched down.

A few yards in front of him was a small, smoky fire, burning near the edge of the reen. Next to it, standing with his back to Conor, a dark-haired man was playing a fiddle. He was playing it quietly now, dreamily, one foot tapping rhythms into the soft mud. The music crooned and hummed in the stillness; the flames crackled on the damp wood.

Who on earth could he be, Conor thought. A tramp? Maybe a gypsy. Whoever he was, he could play. Now the music had slid back to the long eerie notes that wavered and hung, quivered and whispered. It was wonderful music; it dissolved into folk tunes and snatches of half-remembered songs, and before Conor could put names to the tunes they were gone and the fiddler was playing a strange, stately lament, wandering like a shadow through the trees.

Then, as he leaned forward to listen, Conor saw something moving in the grass near the fiddler's feet. It slithered, glinting in the brief moonlight. At first he thought it was an eel that had crawled up out of the reen; then, with a shock, he realized it was water! The green, sluggish water of Marshall's reen was streaming upwards over the bank, forming long, gleaming rivulets that moved silently through the grass. Already a pool was forming behind the fiddler – even as he half turned and started a new tune Conor saw the fingers of water draw back, then trickle out again, sliding ominously after him. It was uncanny. How could water run uphill?

He edged forward, staring. Was it water? He'd

5

thought so, seeing it break and trickle, but now it seemed to him more like a hand; wet fingers reaching for the man's ankle as he played and hummed, his head low over the bow.

Conor jumped up. He shouted. The man's head whipped round. The hand grabbed.

The fiddler jerked back with a screech of his bow; he gave a yell of fury and kicked out at something that glinted and moved at the water's edge, stamping at it in rage, splashing the water high.

'Leave me alone!' he yelled, stumbling backwards. 'Haven't you done enough?'

He was not surprised; he was angry, bitter, shaking with rage. And all at once the water was gone, sinking silently back, sliding soundlessly over the bank into the stagnant reen. All around, the trees stirred their branches.

For a long while the fiddler stood still, as if getting his breath. When he spoke again his voice was calmer. 'For a moment,' he said to the darkness, 'you almost caught me. I didn't think I could come back without you knowing. I'm here to get back what you took from me.'

As if to answer him a terrifying sound rose out of the reen; a thin hiss, a bitter choking. The man waited, warily, until it faded to silence. Then he turned around, to face the trees.

'And who are you?' he asked quietly.

Conor froze. He was sure the man couldn't see him among the branches unless he moved, and he didn't want to be seen either. He wanted to get away from this madness altogether.

But the fiddler pointed his bow at the trees. 'Come on. Show yourself.'

At that moment, to Conor's alarm, the moon drifted from its lid of cloud. It glinted on his face and hands; he saw the man step forward, and in an instant of panic he turned and was running, racing hard over the wet grass, slipping and stumbling, leaping the reeds to the lane and running, running to its end, his bag thumping against him. He turned the corner and hurled himself onto a gate, doubled up and gasping for breath.

For a while the night roared and swung around him, but slowly, as he took great breaths of the damp air, he realized he had not been followed. The lane was silent and dark; the only sounds the drift of voices from the pub just ahead; the slam of a car door. He heaved himself upright and walked wearily up the track.

The Sea Wall Inn was busy; lights blazed from its windows onto the multicoloured row of cars; a few bicycles leaned against the wall. As he walked up to the door and scraped the mud from his boots he thought about the fingers of water that had crawled from the reen. They were quite impossible, of course. But he'd seen them.

2

'So you didn't come home in the bus last night.' His mother lifted the bowl of ferns from the windowsill and scrubbed the faded wood firmly with the duster. Her short dark curtain of hair swung vigorously. He knew she was very angry.

'I did . . . like I said, it broke down. Only up the road. Just beyond Morris's.' It had been further by far, but this was bad enough.

She glared at him over one shoulder. 'You might as well have told me. You know everything gets back to this pub sooner or later.'

He tore the corner off a beer mat, irritably. That was true enough.

'There are some very odd people about these days, Conor. I've got enough to worry about, without you wandering around in the dark.' She straightened, wiping her hand on her cheek and leaving a smudge of dirt. 'Next time, phone me. I don't know why you didn't.' She gave a flick of the duster. 'Evan would have come out and picked you up.'

He glared at her, but she was already back wiping tables. Tossing the beer mat down he swung himself off the stool. 'Can I do anything?'

'Ashtrays, if you like. Or the fires.'

Cleaning the ashtrays was the one job he hated, so today, he told himself, he'd better do it just to keep the peace. He collected them up and emptied all the cigarette ends and ash into the bin. Then he washed them, wiped them carefully, and put them out again, one on each clean table. It was a peaceful thing to do.

The pub was always quietest in the morning. It was a large, rather dark room with small leaded windows on each side of the door. His mother kept it painfully clean; the brass jugs on the shelves gleamed, and every glass shone. A fireplace stood at either end of the room, with an old dark wood mantel shelf and a framed print – Tintern Abbey and Raglan Castle. It had probably been two rooms once – there was a definite rise in the floor halfway across, that strangers carrying drinks often tripped over, soaking their trousers. Now the room was smoky and dim, even in sunlight, smelling of beer and wines and the faintest tang of bacon.

Near the door were the flood marks. The highest was a dim brown smudge higher than his head, with 1863 written next to it in heavy black letters. Below that were eight other lines, at intervals, with a few others almost worn away. Each was dated, in different handwriting; 1908, 1905, 1897, 1966, 1989, this last only about knee-high. That was the only big flood Conor could remember – the tides whipping over the wall, the mud and the sandbags; having to live upstairs for a week. There had been others, of course; water seeped over in most winters and in heavy storms, but they weren't marked. And the house wasn't old enough to have a mark for the Great Flood – that had been in 1606 and had swept whole villages away.

9

In fact, he thought, as he knelt down at the fireplace, the whole house would have been underwater then, and as he shovelled up last night's ashes he imagined fish swimming in at the windows, swirling muddy water and great crusts of barnacles on the tables and chairs.

'Daydreaming, Conor?'

With a jerk he picked up the bucket and looked round. The big man in the doorway smirked at him.

'Oh Evan,' his mother said. 'I'm glad that you're back. The brewer is coming at twelve. Is that all right?'

'Don't you worry. The cellar is all ready.' Evan Lewis sat himself on a clean table, drying his large, hairy hands with a towel.

If I put my feet on the seat like that, Conor thought, she'd say something. Then he told himself fiercely to shut up, and took the cinders out, bringing back sticks and paper and coals.

' . . . It is your birthday after all,' Evan was saying, in a reasoning voice. 'You ought to take the afternoon off. Shouldn't she?' He looked at Conor.

'You mean on Friday?'

'That's right. I thought we could all go to the cinema in Chepstow. My treat.'

Conor made a careful crisscross of sticks on the newspaper.

His mother stood up straight and pushed her hair back. 'That's very kind of you, Evan, but I don't know . . .'

'Please Jill. I'd like to.'

'In any case I wouldn't let you pay. And who'd look after the bar?'

'Nia. Or Siân. They'd do it just for one afternoon.'

10

She put her arms on the bar and leaned her chin on them. 'Well . . . it would be a change. I haven't been to the pictures for ages.'

She looked round at Conor. 'What do you think?'

He put the last piece of coal on the fire and stood up, his hands black. If only he'd thought of this first. Now he was trapped.

'I don't mind.'

'That doesn't sound very keen!'

Conor clenched his fists. 'I mean I'll come, but I'd like to pay for you myself. I've got some money.'

'Wouldn't hear of it.' Evan had poured himself a lemonade shandy and was drinking it noisily.

Conor felt a wave of anger flash over him. 'I don't think you should pay for us,' he snapped. 'It's not as if we're related or anything, is it?'

'Conor!' His mother glared at him. 'Don't be so rude!' She turned. 'Yes, look, Evan we'd be delighted. I'm sure Siân will come in. Thank you very much.'

Damn, thought Conor. Now I've pushed her into it.

'My pleasure.' Evan put down his glass. 'You've got dirt on your face, Jill.' And he took out a clean handkerchief and wiped the smudge off her cheek. She went faintly red.

Conor ground his nails into his palms and turned round, abruptly. A man was standing in the open doorway, watching them.

'Good morning,' he said.

'Morning,' Conor mumbled, in a shocked voice.

He was a young man with a narrow face and black hair. He had a rucksack on his back and a violin-shaped canvas bag under one arm. He gave Conor a cool, considering look.

'We're closed,' Evan said at once.

'I'm sure you are, my friend, but it's not drink I'm after. I've come about the job.'

He put a small piece of paper into Jill's hand. She stared at it vaguely, then her face cleared and she said, 'Oh I see! The advertisement.'

'It's not been filled?'

She turned and smiled at him. 'Not yet. We're looking for someone dependable for a few Tuesday nights, and possibly Saturdays – our live music nights. Just for a while. We usually have a group but the dulcimer player is in hospital and the rest are touring at various folk festivals . . .'

He nodded, and slipped the rucksack off. 'Do you want reels, jigs, ballads? Irish, Welsh?'

'That would be fine.' She hesitated 'Mr . . .?'

'Rhys. But Meurig will do.'

'I suppose you have some references, reviews, that sort of thing?' Evan said, elbowing himself forward. He folded his arms across his broad chest and looked the fiddler up and down. 'We can't employ just anyone. This pub has a name for its music.'

'We!' thought Conor.

The fiddler shrugged. 'I could give a list of people I've played for. But perhaps you should just listen and decide for yourselves.' He took the fiddle out of its bag and drew the bow across, adjusting the pegs. The low squirm of sound reminded Conor of last night. He sat on a stool and waited.

The fiddler did not disappoint him. After five minutes of the sweetest melody she could imagine, his mother came slowly out of her amazement and said 'Do you know that was absolutely wonderful! What was that tune?'

'An air I learned in Brecon once.' The fiddler watched her, his eyes bright. He smiled. 'You love music, I can see.'

'I do indeed, and I've heard plenty, but never anything like that.'

'Look, Jill, this is all very well,' Evan blurted out, 'but you need some references, something . . .'

'No.' She shook her head firmly, 'No I don't. If you can play like that, Meurig, then welcome to The Sea Wall. The regulars will love you.'

He laughed, and began to put the fiddle away. Evan had a glowering look of annoyance, and Conor was glad. Who did he think he was anyway!

'This is my son Conor, and Evan Lewis, our cellarman. Now, have you anywhere to stay?'

The fiddler pulled the cords tight. Then he said 'Yes. The old watchtower on the sea wall belonged to my grandfather. It belongs to me now, though I haven't been there for a while . . .'

'The watchtower?' Conor's mother looked surprised. 'Then I knew your grandfather . . . he came in here sometimes. But can you live there? The sea washes right up to it – around it, at some tides.'

Meurig shrugged. 'I expect so.'

But Conor caught a sudden flicker of unhappiness on the man's face. The memory of the fingers of water groped at him.

'Well if you need any supplies, let me know. You won't be very comfortable there.'

'I'll manage.' Then the fiddler turned to Conor. 'I don't suppose you'd like to help me carry these things down?'

Oh, no, Conor thought, but his mother said, 'Of course he will' with that peculiar threat in her voice

13

that he knew very well, so he carefully picked up the violin bag and followed the fiddler outside.

They walked along the track in silence, skirting the muddy pools. Conor gave a quick glance sideways, and saw that the fiddler was looking at him. Does he know it was me, Conor thought uneasily, or is he just wondering?

But Meurig said nothing. He climbed the steps quickly up to the top of the sea wall, and stood there, his hair and coat lifting and flapping in the wind. Conor climbed up after him.

The Severn was grey and purple; huge, a shifting, breathing mass of water, swollen right up to the base of the wall, lapping quietly. The tide was full and far out the sun glinted on moving threads of current, dark streaks in the water. Beyond, low and faint as cloud, the hills of Somerset glimmered.

About half a mile down the wall was the watch-tower, tall and built of black stone, its windows blank eyes that watched them come.

As they trudged towards it along the muddy path the fiddler said, 'It won't be very dry, I suppose.'

Conor hesitated. Then he said, 'Do you think it will be . . . safe?'

Meuring turned. 'Safe?'

'Yes. You know.'

The fiddler glanced out at the estuary. 'You mean from the water?'

'Yes.'

They looked at each other for a moment. Then the fiddler smiled a bitter smile. 'I doubt it. For me, nowhere is safe, Conor.'

3

The fence was broken, and snagged with debris washed up by the tide; weed, broken boxes, wood, plastic bags. Conor kicked a rotten sack and a crab scuttled out. 'What a mess,' he muttered, watching it.

Meurig had pulled a key out of his pocket and was fitting it into the lock; he had to force it round, grinding into the rust. Even then the door would not open; the wood was swollen and warped. After a few shoves the fiddler pulled his rucksack off and threw it down.

'This will take two of us. Ready?'

They put their shoulders to the door. At the third blow it shuddered ajar, and at the fourth slammed wide, almost pitching Conor onto his face in the dark entry. Echoes hummed through the tower. Upstairs something bumped and slid to the floor.

Meurig stood there, listening.

The building smelt damp; there were pools of water on the floor and the only window was broken, a black spider of cracks sprawling in its glass. Against the curved wall a wooden staircase without a handrail led up into the dark.

'It's like a lighthouse,' Conor muttered.

'Exactly like. But to warn the land against the sea.'

Leaving the door open, the fiddler stepped in. He looked warily up the stairs. The building was quiet, except for the faint sound of dripping.

'Is everything all right?' Conor asked.

The fiddler gave him an odd look. 'Can you hear that?'

Far above them, something was moving. It slithered, wet and heavy, over a stone floor.

'What is it?'

Meurig didn't answer, but moved a few steps up, into dimness. Conor followed, one hand on the damp wall. They listened, their breath a faint mist.

The dragging stopped.

Meurig began to climb, quietly, with Conor close behind, his heart thudding. The steps were steep and slippery, they wound up around the wall, passing a few narrow windows clogged with dirt and salt. Rubbing one with his finger he saw the estuary below, gleaming brown and silver as the tide flooded it, and some gulls and oystercatchers on the thin line of wet mud. He stepped up, and banged into Meurig.

'Listen.'

There was the dripping; louder now, a slow rhythmic plopping into some pool. And again that slow, indefinable slither, high in a room above.

Conor shivered. 'Do you know what it is?'

'It's water,' the fiddler said, grimly.

Conor shot a look at him. The man's face was a pale glimmer in the dark, a wary stillness. Conor bit his lip, and then jerked with sudden terror as something icy splatted on his cheek. Putting up his hand he felt wetness, and breathed out through gritted teeth, but when he reached up to brush the roof it was dry. Quite dry.

They went up again, step by step. After a while they came to a door on the right: Meurig opened it gently and let it swing wide.

This room had some furniture, a table, chairs, a sink. Water dripping from the ceiling had made an ugly green stain down the wall. There was a smell of mould.

'She's taken this tower,' Meurig said, 'and it's all my fault.'

'Who has?'

But the fiddler was looking up at the ceiling. Water dripped from the middle of it, onto the table.

Upstairs must be awash, Conor thought; the roof had probably gone. 'You can't live here. Come back to the Inn.'

'It's a lot better than the place I've come from.' Abruptly Meurig turned and ran up to the top room. As his fingers closed on the latch he paused, and again Conor heard from inside that peculiar drift and swish of sound, and suddenly it reminded him of a dress, a long, wet dress, dragging along the floor.

'She won't keep me out,' Meurig muttered. He flung the door open; Conor flinched, expecting a wave, a tide of water to come rushing out and sweep them down the stairs. But the room was perfectly dry. And empty.

It was a circular room, with windows all around, full of sunlight. Meurig walked in. 'Yes I'm back,' he said.

He turned to Conor who was staring at the dry floorboards, and smiled, as if he was relieved. 'Well, this isn't too bad, is it? At least it's habitable.'

17

There was a small bare wooden bed opposite; cupboards, a shelf and a clutter of rubbish – a few boxes, some old newspapers, a broken chair. Conor came in, cautiously. Someone had been in here, he was sure. A tang of salt hung in the air; one window banged open. He turned a complete circle, staring out: the sea, the Levels, the hills, a far horizon right around. 'What a view.'

Crossing to the open window he caught the handle and found it wet. A slither of water ran over the sill and down the wall outside, leaving a green stain. Conor touched it, puzzled.

'It was to watch for flooding?'

'That's right.' Meurig had thrown his rucksack down and was rummaging through the boxes. 'There was always a flood warden – they were paid, long ago, by the monastery, and then by the parish. After that, they did it for nothing. Generation after generation. My grandfather was the last. He lived up here until about two years ago – don't you remember him?'

Conor thought he did – a dark, silent man sitting in the corner of the pub. 'Yes, I was a bit scared of him. I was only a kid, mind.'

Meurig nodded. 'He was a grim man. It does that to you, watching Hafren.' He stood up, and nodded at the window. 'It's a war Conor, between her and us.' He gazed down at the estuary, all the glinting miles of tide. 'She wants the land and we won't let her have it.'

'You talk as if the river were alive.'

Meurig looked at him sidelong. 'Because she is.'

Conor was picking through the litter on the windowsill. He didn't like Meurig making fun of him. 'So where have you been these last two years then?'

'That's my business,' the fiddler snapped. 'Do you think I've been . . . My God, DON'T TOUCH THAT!'

He was across the room in an instant; he had snatched the candle stub out of Conor's hand before Conor could move.

'It's only a candle!' Conor gasped. 'An old candle! That's all! What on earth's the matter?'

The fiddler closed shaking fingers round it tight. For a long moment he said nothing. Then he said, 'I'm sorry. For a moment I thought it was something else.'

'What?' Conor snapped. 'Dynamite?'

Meurig gave him a hurt, bitter smile. 'Clever.'

He went over and opened a window and leaned out, hands on the sill, the wind ruffling his hair. He looked quite sick, and Conor, watching him, suddenly felt sorry. After a moment he went and stood next to him. He wanted to say something kind, but couldn't.

'Last night,' he said, looking towards the pub, 'I heard you playing.'

'I know you did.' The fiddler leaned back against the window and looked at him. Conor waited for an explanation, but it didn't come. Instead the fiddler turned his light green eyes back to the window and said, 'Tell me about the houses I can see. Who lives in them, these days?'

Conor shrugged. 'The same, mostly. That's Ty Gwyn, the Mostyns have farmed there for years . . . and Jack Morris and his mother live over there at Monk's Acre . . .'

'What about the house in the trees?'

'That's been empty for a few months but there's a man called John Caristan moving in now. He used to be my teacher when I was little, but he's retired these days. Came into money, my mother says. He collects antiques.'

The fiddler gazed intently at the slate roof, half visible through the blown branches. 'Caristan.'

'Yes. Do you know him?'

Meurig didn't answer. Instead he said, 'And who's this, on the bike?'

A girl was riding along the top of the sea wall from the direction of the pub, her hair blown over her eyes by the wind. Conor looked down.

'That's Sara Mostyn. She lives at the farm. I expect she's looking for me.'

It seemed she knew where to look too, he thought, watching her jerk to a halt outside the broken fence and wave up at the window, tugging hair from her eyes and mouth. He leaned out. 'Wait there. I'll be right down.'

'Well hurry up. We're late.'

He turned to the fiddler. 'I've got to go. We promised to help Mr Caristan unpack – he's not very fit and his stuff is coming today. I'll see you in the pub?'

'Surely.'

Conor paused at the door and looked back. Meurig was still leaning against the window, looking out.

'Are you sure,' Conor said awkwardly, 'that you're all right?'

Meurig glanced down at the candle stub still in his hand. Then he threw it wearily into a box in the corner. 'I'm all right Conor. For the moment.'

4

'What about here?'

'No . . .' John Caristan ran a hand through his dusty hair. 'Sara, what do you think?'

'I think it would look better on that little table.'

With a sigh, Conor moved the vase again.

'Oh yes,' Mr Caristan said, 'that's it. What would I do without you. Now the books – they go in the other room.' He picked up a box and went out with it, peering carefully round the sides for obstacles.

'So go on. Did he say why?' Sara asked, unwrapping another vase from newspaper.

'Not really.' Conor perched on the arm of a chair, and wound a piece of string round his fingers. 'He just snatched it out of my hand as if it was going to explode. Then he said he'd thought it was something else.'

'What?'

'Exactly. But I'll tell you what Sara, he was terrified. He looked really ill.'

She frowned, tucking her hair behind one ear. 'Just a candle?'

'Yes.'

'He sounds weird.'

'I don't know.' He swung his foot, wondering whether to tell her about the fingers of water that had groped from the reen. Maybe not yet.

'Oh look at this, Conor. It must be worth a fortune!'

Out of the paper came a large Chinese jar, its sides glittering with strange pagodas and ladies in long, swaying poses.

'Not quite a fortune.' Mr Caristan came in with a tea-tray and set it down unsteadily on a packing case. 'Might take a few years' pocket money though. Do children still call it pocket money, these days?'

They laughed, and exchanged awkward looks.

'Sometimes,' Conor said. He never knew whether or not to add 'Sir'. It sounded odd either way.

'Now that box,' Caristan said, nodding at it as he handed out a mug of hot chocolate, 'has some interesting things. Staffordshire pieces, some Meisen, the best of my Chelsea. Chelsea's my speciality – I collect it. Gorgeous stuff. Thin as eggshell.'

He dumped a spoonful of sugar in the mug and handed it to Sara.

'Do you eat off them?' she asked.

'Good Lord, no!'

'Then what's the point? I mean,' she tapped the jar lightly with her spoon, 'it must be such a worry, in case they get broken, or stolen. I drop cups and plates all the time.'

'Do you indeed?' A small frown creased his forehead; he picked up the Chinese jar smoothly and slid it onto a shelf. 'Good heavens, Sara, what a revelation to make. That doesn't do my blood pressure any good, I can tell you.'

'Well, not quite all the time.'

He sat down and stretched out his legs. 'I'm glad to hear it! The point, Sara, is that they are very beautiful objects, and I just like looking at them. And they're old, of course; from a time when things were made more carefully, by hand, not by machines. I like that. From a money point of view, they can be a bit of a worry. Hence insurance. And the burglar alarm. Have a biscuit, Conor.'

Conor took a chocolate digestive gratefully. He never got them at home.

'Sara?'

'No thanks. They rot your teeth.'

'You have sugar, though?'

'That's different.' She sipped from her mug thoughtfully. 'I saw you had an alarm. It must have cost a bit.'

'I can afford it now. And I deserve it, after all those years of drudgery in school!'

He looked comically at them and they both laughed, but Conor thought he meant it. He could remember Mr Caristan's class, years ago now; the constant noise, the class toughs being cheeky and uncontrollable, ignoring the timid 'Please sit down boys'. There had been one day when the headmaster had come in and roared at them all in fury. And Conor had caught Mr Caristan's look; a mixture of embarrassment and shame and bewilderment that he had never forgotten. No, Mr Caristan hadn't been a very good teacher. He must be very relieved to be out of it.

But Sara was still thinking about the china. 'Have you ever been burgled?' she asked.

Caristan looked unhappy. 'Once. About two years ago, when I lived in Chepstow.'

'What happened?'

'Oh, it wasn't very pleasant. The man was caught. I had a dog then, an Alsatian, dear old Marcus. He pinned the fellow against the wall, bit his hand too. A neighbour heard all the noise and came in. Then it was the police and the court . . . all pretty unsavoury. I almost felt for the thief, in the end.'

They were quiet a moment. The wind rattled a loose pane of glass. 'I must get that fixed,' Caristan said, absently.

Sara put down her mug and looked at her watch. 'I'll have to go home,' she said. 'It's five o'clock.'

Mr Caristan sighed, and gazed hopelessly at the stack of packing cases still blocking the hall. 'I suppose you must. Didn't get very far, did we?'

'Sara's fault,' Conor said, 'wanting to know the value of everything.'

'A collector in the making, I can see.'

'We'll come again,' she said, 'promise.'

'I'd be grateful.' Mr Caristan heaved himself up. 'I'll walk home with you both. Doctor says walk a leisurely mile a day. I won't say I might not linger in the Sea Wall, either, for a well-earned half. We'll need an umbrella, though.'

He was right. Conor was surprised at how the light had faded outside; a great mass of dark cloud was streaming in over the estuary, with a few white birds wheeling and gliding under it. Black-headed gulls, he thought, and a few terns. The fields looked bleak; the small bent trees seeming to huddle before the rising wind. Rain was already drizzling; before they had reached the corner of the lane it was a heavy downpour, pattering on Conor's hood and Caristan's umbrella, as he struggled to hold it over Sara and himself.

'Take it with you,' he said to her at the top of the drive to Ty Gwyn, but she shook her head and climbed onto the bicycle.

'Can't. Get blown off. See you tomorrow!'

And she was away, wobbling down the rutted track, the wind sending her hair out like a pennant.

'Mad girl!' Caristan called out.

Conor grinned. 'She's that all right.'

Turning, he saw the watchtower, stark against the growing storm. A thin wisp of smoke streamed from the chimney. Meurig must have found some dry wood, at least, before the rain.

The Sea Wall Inn was a haven on autumn evenings like this. Light gleamed from every window; when you opened the door and came in, dripping with rain and windblown, you felt the thick stone walls close around you, solid and safe.

Although it was early it was already warm; the two fires were crackling over their sticks and sea-coal, and a few old men sat round a table discussing live-stock prices.

Mr Caristan heaved his raincoat off. 'What a sanctuary!' He hung it on a peg and came over and leaned on the bar, where Evan Lewis was polishing glasses. 'A half, Evan please, of your best.'

Conor left them to it and went through to the back.

'Your tea's ready,' his mother said crisply, 'but get those wet things off.'

Upstairs, he changed and then looked out of the window. Here the wall loomed close against the sky; it was higher than the house, green with slippery grass. On the other side, invisible, was the river, black by now, with the lights of Clevedon reflecting faintly. It would be ebbing, swiftly, soundlessly pulling back its power. He remembered what Meurig had said. Hafren was the name for the river – Severn in English, or Sabrina, the Romans' name for her, the goddess or the drowned princess in the water. Fierce, eager to drown and flood. So the fingers then, had been hers . . . the same, he thought, that scraped at the wall night after night, fingering the piled-up rocks and the great cement foundations. It was all crazy – except that he had seen them.

Then he saw the fiddler. Meurig was coming up the track towards the pub, hands in pockets, head bent against the wind. Conor ran downstairs, and found him in the kitchen.

'I can let you have some milk,' his mother was saying, 'and tea. Cheese, if you want it. No bread, I'm afraid, I'll need that for sandwiches – there's a darts match later . . . oh, well, maybe a few slices won't hurt.'

The fiddler smiled wryly at her. 'Thanks.'

'Will that be enough?'

'Plenty. I'll walk up to the shop at Pye Corner tomorrow.'

He glanced at Conor, and pulled some money out of his pocket. 'The weather's turned bad.'

'Perhaps you brought it with you.' She handed him some change and Conor noticed his wary look.

'Perhaps I did.'

As they went out through the bar Conor said, 'I don't think I'd fancy spending the night out there, especially tonight.'

Meurig shrugged and went out into the porch. 'It suits me.'

They stood there a moment, listening to the rain hissing on the fields and trees.

26

'Conor,' the fiddler said suddenly, 'did you go to see your friend, the one with the antiques?'

'Yes. Why?'

'What does he collect?'

Conor frowned. 'China. Chelsea, some of it.'

'Plates and cups? Candlesticks?'

'That sort of thing. Why?'

Meurig shrugged. 'I just wouldn't think it would be safe. He's got a dog, I suppose.'

'No. But he's got a burglar alarm.'

The fiddler stepped out into the rain. 'I'm glad to hear it. You'd better get inside. Your tea will be cold. Goodnight.'

'Goodnight.' But Conor stayed where he was, watching the man become a shadow moving into the squall, and then nothing. Now what was all that about? Meurig had wanted to know something. And, he thought, I think I've told him, without even knowing.

As he turned in the doorway he paused. In the darkness outside, just to his left, something had moved. There was a faint rustle and drip. Conor stood still, his heart hammering.

He came back out into the rain. It lashed into his eyes and down his chin, but he waited, listening. There were some bushes and brambles in the corner, and beyond them a reen, smothered with willows that hung over it. Now the wind moved the dark branches, making them sway and hunch and hiss. Behind him, from the pub, came the hum of voices, and the comforting light that streamed out, throwing his enormous shadow out from his feet. But he felt cold, afraid. The sound was behind him now; a choking hiss, and then, distinctly, a ripple of cold laughter. His hands clenched.

'Conor. Over here Conor.'

It was a fluid, cold voice, as if the rain had spoken, or something underwater had bubbled the words out.

He jumped back, quickly. Next minute he was in the porch, slamming the door behind him. He was wet and shivering, trying to think, but there was no time for that either, because Mr Caristan was there, watching him anxiously.

'Conor,' he said, 'I think I'd better have a word with your mother. Is that all right?'

Bewildered, Conor nodded. 'Yes . . . I suppose so. She's in the kitchen.'

Leading him through he was struck by the change in Mr Caristan. He looked worried, even afraid. Surely he hadn't heard the voice too? When they were in the kitchen Mr Caristan said, 'I'm sorry Jill, but it's important I have a word. Alone, I'm afraid.'

'Take this,' Conor's mother said to him frostily.

He picked up his plate and went into the bar, but thought absently about a knife and fork and turned back. As he reached the door he paused. It was ajar, and Caristan was talking, in a quick, embarrassed way. '. . . and it's not that I'd want to stand in his way Jill, not if he's making a new life for himself, but I just felt you ought to know, if he hasn't told you himself. I mean, he'd be in the bar, where there's money, and there's Conor to think of.'

'He hasn't told me anything,' Conor heard his mother say grimly. 'What has he done then?'

'Well . . .' Mr Caristan sounded unhappy, but firm, 'the fact is, that the man I just saw in the bar, Meurig Rhys, is a thief. He attempted to rob me two years ago, and was caught. In fact Jill, I should imagine that he's only just got out of prison.'

5

The sky over the church was grey; heavy with unfallen rain. As Conor glanced up at it he saw the weather vane creak round and back in the wind that spun leaves down on his face. Already the base of the wall where he sat was clogged with a wet, golden drift of them. He swished them absently with his feet.

'She was shocked, I suppose. So was I. I mean, that he'd been in prison! Then, after she'd thought about it, she said if he'd had his punishment no one should give him any more, least of all her.'

'So he's keeping the job?'

'Looks like it. I think she'll tell him she knows, though.'

Sara pulled a leaf out of her hair and dropped it on a gravestone. 'I like your mother. She's her own person.'

Conor laughed. 'You say some daft things. Whose person would she be?'

'She might be yours. She might even be Evan's.'

He glared at her. 'Him! Why him?'

'Oh, I'm only teasing, Conor.' Sara smiled her most smug smile. 'And anyway, you're the daft one. I don't know why you let him worry you. Anyone can see she's not interested in him.'

Conor turned his head and jumped down off the wall into the leaves. He put his hands in his pockets and strode off towards the church. With a sigh Sara slid down and went after him. 'Don't get all moody on me.'

'I'm not. I'm thinking.' He kicked a stone into the long grass and a frog croaked, unexpectedly. 'Listen, don't you think it's strange that Meurig has come back here?'

'He lives here.'

'Yes . . . but he was asking about Caristan. I wish I hadn't told him so much – he must think I'm a real find. I even told him about the Chelsea stuff, and about the alarm. Do you think he's going to try again?'

'You know him, not me.'

Conor shook his head. 'I can't believe he's a thief. He's odd, but I think he's worried over something.'

They paused by the stone flood mark on the church wall and looked up at it.

'You'll just have to tell him,' Sara said firmly. 'Tell him you know that Caristan recognized him. That's all.'

Conor nodded, reading the words on the stone, as he had often done before.

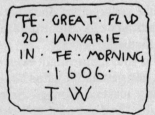

```
TE · GREAT · FLUD
20 · IANVARIE
IN · TE · MORNING
· 1606 ·
   T W
```

It reminded him. 'That's not all.'

'What?'

He told her, as carefully as he could, about the fingers of water that had groped from the reen, about the fiddler's anger and fear. Even as he said it he knew it sounded wild, as if he had imagined it in the dark, among the eeriness of the fiddle-wail. But she listened. And when he'd finished, she didn't say anything for a while. That was one thing he liked about her; she never said the first thing that came into her head. He knew she was turning it over, just as she twisted the one long strand of brown hair round her finger.

'It's an old idea,' she said at last, 'about the river, the spirit of the river, being alive and hungry. The Severn takes three lives a year, they say.'

He nodded, as they walked down to the gate. 'Yes but Meurig talks as if it's . . . she's real. And then there was last night.'

'What about it?'

'After he'd gone I heard something . . . someone laughing. A low, creepy laugh. From the reen. And someone said my name.'

Sara looked at him quickly, but his face was serious.

'It could have been anyone.'

They opened the rusty gate and trooped through, letting it clang behind them.

'Right then.' Sara spun around suddenly in the path. 'I'm coming with you. I think it's about time we found out what this Meurig's up to. Come on.'

The lane from the church to the sea wall ran between open fields, with the usual narrow green-coated reen on either side. A few stunted willows leaned at angles. Cows lifted their heads and watched Conor and Sara walk silently by; two cars slithered past them on the wet road. It began to rain again, and the horizon closed in, misty and blurred. When they climbed the steps to the wall they were wet already, and Conor's hands were cold with the water that ran down them.

The Severn lay churning in its shoals and currents. They knew how immense its power was. Almost the greatest tidal sweep in the world surged through it twice a day, an enormous weight of water pouring from the heart of the sea, scraping and scouring the long banks of chocolate-grey mud, roaring in at over eight miles an hour, sweeping away everything.

Now the tide was out. Before them a great scatter of birds picked and waded on the treacherous flats, daintily probing, walking with long toes that left light prints. Curlews cried, out there on the waterline; knots, dunlin, oystercatchers and gulls rose in clouds, crying and settling. Half-sunk in the mud were old groynes, and the hulks of rotten boats that the tides had bleached and split until they looked more like rock than wood; strange, petrified forms. Conor watched the birds, wishing he had his binoculars.

'Gulls,' Sara remarked.

'Black-headed. Lots of other species too.'

'I can't see any black heads.'

'It's only in summer the heads are black. Now they've just got a dot behind the eye. You can see it on that one, over there.'

'Conor,' she said, in a strained voice, 'there's someone out there.'

He looked where she pointed among the wheeling birds. Right on the water line, knee-deep in the mud, a woman was standing. She had her back to them, and was looking out at the purple-grey water; a wave ran in and lapped about her.

'What's she doing!' Sara breathed. 'She'll get stuck!'

Almost as if she had heard, the woman turned her head, looking back towards them. She wore a grey dress that seemed to drift in the tide; her hair was dark and long, blown by the wind.

A squall of rain blurred between them. Birds swirled. Then the shoreline was empty.

For a moment they both stood there, astonished, while the rain splattered into a pool at their feet. Then Sara shook her head. 'Where did she go? Let's go down.'

They ran down the steep concrete steps; at the bottom the thin stretch of shingle was scattered with black masses of drying seaweed. Down here in the hush they could hear the faint popping and bubbling of the mud, an enormous expanse stretching from the Porton Grounds to Goldcliff Point, all empty, except for the rain and the picking, wheeling flocks.

Conor put his boot into the mud; it sank and was held, gently. The mud was almost liquid.

'No one could possibly have stood out there.'

Sara shrugged, bewildered. 'Maybe there's a sand-bank . . .'

'There isn't. You know that. And where did she go? Into the water?'

Sara looked at him. 'She disappeared, didn't she. Into nowhere.'

Before they came to the watchtower the sound of the fiddle drifted out to meet them, and Conor noticed again the peculiar tone it had, purer and clearer than any other. He wondered if Sara had noticed; as they walked towards the building he saw she was listening, but neither of them spoke.

Conor banged on the door. The music stopped; Meurig opened a window and looked down.

'This is Sara,' Conor said.

'I remember. Come up, it's not locked.'

When they walked breathlessly into the top room he was putting the fiddle away, wrapping it carefully. 'Damp,' he said absently, 'makes the strings slack.'

Sara looked round, curiously. A fire crackled in the swept hearth; next to it was a stack of driftwood in various stages of drying, faint steam rising from it. A few chairs and the table had been brought up; the bed, with a neat sleeping bag on it, stood against one wall.

'Sit down.' Meurig looked sideways at them.

'Sorry about the mud.'

'That doesn't matter. I tramp in enough myself.'

The fire was a fierce heat; after a moment Sara edged her chair away. Meurig came over and sat on the hearth.

'How are you managing?' Conor said, after an awkward pause.

'Fine, thanks. I walked to Redwick this morning and bought some things – enough to keep me going.' Meurig was watching them closely. 'What's troubling you, Conor?' he said softly.

Conor looked helplessly at Sara.

'You should tell him,' she said.

'Tell me what?'

Conor felt the heat rise in his face. He untwisted his fingers. 'We know,' he muttered. 'I mean, about the burglary . . . and everything.'

For a moment Meurig was very still. Then he put

his arms around his knees and stared bleakly across the room. The silence was terrible; Conor had to fill it. 'Mr Caristan recognized you.'

'So I gather.' Meurig's voice was harsh. 'When?'

'Last night, in the pub.'

'I didn't see him.'

'He was standing at the bar.'

The fiddler turned his head away. 'I presume he's told your mother?'

Conor nodded.

'So that's it, then.'

'No it's not,' Sara said. 'Tell him, go on.'

'Well . . . I overheard. I mean, they don't know we know. My mother told Caristan that it doesn't matter as far as she's concerned. She still wants you to play.'

'Does she now?' Meurig gave them a wan smile. 'She's a good one, your mother.'

Conor was annoyed. 'It's true then? You were in prison? You should have told her if you thought she was so good.'

After a moment Meurig got up and went to the window. 'I'm not a thief, Conor, no matter who says so. I suppose you thought I'd come to try again.'

'We didn't know . . .'

'Don't lie, Conor.' The fiddler turned. 'This is to warn me off, right?'

Angry now, Conor jumped up. 'Yes, all right! Don't try to use me, that's all. I like Mr Caristan. I don't want him robbed!'

'Neither do I.' Meurig took a tense step towards him. 'But he's got something I need. Something of mine.'

'Yours?'

'And I want you to help me get it back.'

35

Conor turned abruptly. 'No, I don't believe you. Come on, Sara.'

She took a step and stopped. 'Hey, I'm not on a lead, you know. I think we should wait, Conor.'

He glared at her. 'You believe all this?'

'I might, if I had a chance to hear it.'

'Listen,' Meurig said quietly, 'it's true Conor, I swear it. It's vital to me.'

Conor looked at him. 'So what's he got of yours that's so precious?'

The fiddler shrugged. 'You might say he's got my soul.'

6

They sat close together, around the fire. A squall of rain rattled the window; the sky darkened under the gathering cloud.

'There's always been a watchtower,' Meurig began, 'and a watcher, ever since the monks first took the land from the river, drained it, dug the reens, built the first wall. Year after year, one family, and when they died out, another. My grandfather was the last. Since then no one has watched her. I should have been here to take his place.'

He pushed a twig deep into the fire.

'What about your father?' Sara asked.

He shook his head. 'No, both my parents were dead by then. There was only me. And I was away, in Scotland . . . but I've gone too fast. The whole thing started long before then. It started the night after I was born.'

He looked at them. 'My grandfather told me what happened. It was in a house near here, down towards Magor. And it was a night like this one coming; dark, wet, and with a raging tide. There was a party, a celebration. The tower was left empty; my grandfather came, my parents' friends, there was a crowd in the house. The windows were open, moths and spray and leaves fluttering in. There was music too, fiddles and whistles, and all the house was lit up with candles and lamps.

'Late in the evening, they started the blessing. It's an old thing, a custom on the Levels; they passed a jug around and everyone drank and wished something on the baby – luck, good health, you know the sort of thing.'

Conor nodded, imagining the hot, bright, crowded room.

'Well,' Meurig went on, slowly, 'there was a woman in the corner, a dark-haired woman in a green dress. No one had noticed her, particularly. When it came to her turn she drank, and put the jug down. Then she pointed her finger at a candle that was burning on the chimney shelf. She said "The child's life will end if the candle burns away.'

They stared at him.

'A candle?' Sara said.

'That's right,' Meurig gave them a sideways look. 'It was before I was christened, you see . . . I suppose there was uproar, confusion. When they tried to grab her she was gone. The floor was awash; the tide had risen to the top of the wall and was swirling in at the door. In all the hubbub my grandfather snatched up the candle and blew it out.'

He frowned, rubbing his forehead. 'He kept it. Once or twice he showed it to me, but usually he kept it locked up, somewhere secret. I remember it was just an ordinary white candle, a few inches high. He tied a red thread round it, so as not to get it mixed up with any other, and he kept it safe. He believed in her curse, you see.'

Sara shook her head. 'It's impossible. Life can't depend on something else.'

'She has power for that, Sara. She locked my soul in that thing.'

'You mean,' Conor said, 'that if someone burnt it away, you'd just . . .'

'Die.' Meurig finished quietly. 'Such things have happened before. There are spells, curses, words that will work themselves out, because of the will of the sayer. She came for my great grandfather – drowned him miles inland. And then there was Carys Rhys, in the last century – Hafren cursed her that she should never see her wedding day. Nor did she. A wave washed her from the wall the night before it. No one even knew why she was out there.' He watched the fire sombrely. 'And have you ever thought how a candle is like a life? That the flame moves like something living, that it's warm and quick, and then it eats itself away until quite suddenly it's gone, nowhere, leaving nothing.'

'I hadn't thought of it,' Conor said.

'I have. I've had plenty of time.'

'But mightn't it work the other way?' Sara interrupted. 'I mean that as long as the candle's safe you will live?'

'Live for ever?' Conor muttered.

Meurig shook his head. 'She didn't say that, though it might have been a heavier curse than the other. No she just gave me an extra danger – burning that candle. Anyway we'll never really know, will we, unless we light it and let it burn.'

'You're hardly likely to do that!' Sara muttered.

'I can't.' Meurig shook his head bitterly. 'I've lost it.'

'Lost it!'

'In a way. I think I know where it is, but I can't get at it.'

'But you mean anyone could light it . . .'

'Exactly.' Meurig watched the flames. 'That's all I seem to have thought about these two years. Locked up in that cell, fretting, counting the hours . . . knowing I just might stop, go out, as if a hand had clenched over me . . .'

Conor went from astonishment to sudden understanding. 'It's at Caristan's! That's why you tried to rob him!'

'That's right,' Meurig said. He rubbed his cheek with one long finger. 'You see when my grandfather died I came back from Scotland, where I'd been playing, cleared my cottage, and sold it to move here. This was where I had to be. Then when I moved into the watchtower, I sorted through my grandfather's things and took a crate of bits and pieces to a junk stall in Chepstow market. Two days later I found a letter from him; it was about the candle. He told me it was in a small gilt box, and I knew that it was too late. The box had been in with all that stuff. I'd looked in it, and thought it was empty, but there's a secret drawer – the candle was in there.'

'What did you do?' Conor asked.

'What do you think! I was there next morning when the market opened, but the box was gone. Sold. Caristan had bought it, but it took me days to find out who he was and where he lived – then I went to his house.' He frowned. 'I was worried. Panicky. The place was dark; I thought he was out. The window was open. I thought it would be quick, and easy.'

He laughed bitterly. 'I was stupid. Ten minutes

later I was pinned to the wall by a dog, covered in blood, with the neighbours in and the police on their way.'

'Didn't you try to explain?'

Meurig eyed him coldly. 'For a while. Until I got sick of their sarcasm.'

They were silent. It had gone dark in the room, and quite cold. Meurig got up and brought the lamp to the table. He turned up the wick and lit it with a spill from the fire.

'So that's my problem' he said. 'I can't go there again, obviously. I need your help.'

'We'll do it,' Sara said, immediately. She looked at Conor.

'Steal the candle?' he said.

'And replace it with another. He'll never know the difference, even if he's found it.'

Conor thought about it. It didn't sound too difficult. 'All right. But look, why don't you just ask him for it . . . explain it to him, I mean. He's a kindly old man . . .'

Meurig shook his head firmly. 'I tried that last time. No one believed me – why should they? And Caristan already thinks I'm a thief and a liar and probably half mad. You heard how he warned your mother. No, Conor, I can't face that. I need you to try and get it for me. Otherwise I don't know what I'll do.'

'We'll do it,' Sara said. 'We've said so, haven't we?' She scrambled up, pulling the hair from her face. 'Don't worry Meurig. It'll be no problem.'

That night Conor lay in bed, watching the thin moon outside his window, and listening to the music of the fiddle. Downstairs in the hot, noisy bar, Meurig was playing a set of reels; dancing music, that made you want to leap and shout; fierce music, full of energy. When it was finished there was a roar of voices, a beating of tables, applause. He was going down well. Conor rolled over. He felt warm, and sleepy. He was used to the voices downstairs, they were there every night, they never kept him awake. In fact they were comforting. He thought about the candle, lying in its dusty box somewhere in the muddle at Caristan's house, forgotten. Or what if it had been sold, or even found and thrown out, in some dustbin, some rubbish tip, nibbled by rats? He closed his eyes. The music had begun again without his noticing. Slow now, and dreamy, it led him deep into sleep.

Late in the night, he dreamed. Someone was tapping at his window. Turning on the pillow, he pushed the hair from his eyes and saw her, the woman from the mud flats, her long dark hair floating out, her green eyes close to the window.

'Let me in Conor,' she said quietly.

He sat up, and swung his legs out into the cold. In the dark room the gleaming hands of the clock whirled crazily round and round. He walked to the window. Water was seeping in through the gaps around the frame; a green trickle of it ran down the wall.

'Let me in,' she hissed, her face against the glass.

Reluctantly, he reached out his hands, and noticed they were wearing Sara's red gloves. Then he seized the window, and heaved it up.

The river exploded into the room, pouring in a smooth green torrent over his feet. Looking out he saw it was high over the sea wall, a glassy lake that roared in, bringing mud and drowned birds and eels and broken nets and all the debris of the estuary. It rose around him quickly up to the ceiling; he was in a cube of water, but he could walk and breath without surprise, so he went over and opened the bedroom door and drifted downstairs.

The bar was drowned and silent; fish swam through it. Chairs and tables hung, lifted at strange angles. He stood there a moment, his hand on the door, watching weed wave from the chimney, a small crab scuttling across the silted floor. Beer mats floated around him like flatfish, advertisements for Guiness stamped on their bellies. Tiny eels slid between his fingers.

She was sitting at a table near the window. For a moment she looked an old, old woman, but even as he looked her face blurred and she was young, her dress green with weed and crusts of shellfish. She beckoned to him with a long hand.

'Come and see what I've brought you, Conor.'

On the table, burning in the murky water, was a white candle. The flame rose, long and smoky, and Hafren watched it, her eyes lit with its glow, weeds and bubbles rising from her hair. It was Meurig's candle.

'Put it out!' he whispered.

She put her finger into the flame. 'Ah but I can't. I've lit it, and now I can never put it out.'

A fish swam past Conor's ear. 'Spells and curses,' it murmured. 'Words that work themselves out.'

'Put it out, please!' He could feel the heat now, burning inside him, he was hot and melting, losing himself, losing all strength. He flung himself forward, floundered, swam, struggled so hard that the bedclothes fell off him and he sat up, suddenly cold.

He waited, heart thudding.

The room was quiet; it was long after closing time. He leaned over and pulled the blankets back onto the bed. Then, quickly, he got out and crossed to the window, avoiding the creaking board so that his mother wouldn't hear him.

The window was closed tight. Outside, the great black bank of the wall rose up, high against the sky. Far along it, one light gleamed in the watchtower. He watched it for a while, oddly comforted.

7

'Slow down, Conor!' Sara bumped the bicycle over the rough track. 'If you don't I'll get on and ride there.'

Conor stopped his grim march and stared out at the pale blue sky.

'That's better.' She caught up and took out a packet of mints and handed him one. He ate it, without looking at her.

'It's Evan,' he said, after a while.

'I should have guessed!'

He gave her an angry look and walked on. 'He's found out about Meurig.'

Sara lifted her eyebrows. 'Your mother told him?'

'No. Someone in the bar. It's got round already. That made it worse, of course . . . he went on and on. Why hadn't she told him? Why were they employing a thief? They!' He kicked a stone in an explosion of fury. 'It's our pub, not his. I'm sick of him!'

After a while she said, 'They had a row, then?'

'Not even that.' Conor shoved his hands in his pockets. 'He doesn't argue with you, he just . . .' he shrugged, 'oh, you know, he just goes on, in a reasonable whine. Meurig might steal things, he can't be trusted, they should have insisted on references . . . sickening.'

She nodded, 'Well, look, forget it. It's not worth it. I take it Meurig's staying?'

'Oh yes. She says it's her decision.'

'And you worry about her! Now, did you get a candle?'

He brought it out from his pocket. 'From the box under the sink.'

'And I've got one too, so that whichever of us finds it can just swap and no fuss.' She grinned. 'I'll be like that spy in the film last night. Beautiful and clever.'

Conor snorted.

They walked slowly up to Caristan's house. The red creeper that massed all over the front had left a rich scatter of leaves on the path. They crunched through them to the door and rang the bell. Sara nudged Conor. 'See the alarm?'

While he was looking up at it the door opened.

'Hello!' Mr Caristan was wiping his hands on an old yellow duster; his face lit up when he saw them.

'We just thought . . .' Conor began. He glanced at Sara.

'. . . you'd still need our help,' she finished, brightly.

'Absolutely! There are about three hundred books in here, all over the place. Put the bike round the back, in the shed.'

Conor wiped his feet on the mat and took his coat off, looking around. The house was in an even worse state than a few days ago. The remains of Mr Caristan's midday meal – fish and chips by the look of it – stood on a packing case. He whipped it into the bin at once.

'My books,' he said, waving a hand.

'Why are they all over the floor?' Conor muttered.

'Well, I started sorting them, you know, but I kept dipping in, reading this and that – then I look up and whole hours have gone.' He smiled at Sara as she came in. 'And I simply have to have a few cups of tea to keep me going . . .'

They laughed.

'Well we'll soon sort it out,' Sara said, with a quick glance at Conor.

'I hear,' Mr Caristan said quietly, 'that your mother's keeping her fiddler.'

Conor nodded. 'Yes.'

Mr Caristan shook his head. 'Well I hope she knows what she's doing. He's a strange young man. He said such odd things.'

Conor frowned at Sara. He could see Meurig had been right. Caristan would have laughed away any story about a candle.

They stacked the books and put them on the shelves, flicking each with a duster. Caristan wandered in and out, fetching more, talking, reading them favourite poems, launching into speeches about M R James and Dafydd ap Gwilym. After a while they just wished he would go, but knew they'd have to put up with him. Sara offered to make tea, and when she brought the tray in, at least half an hour later, she gave Conor a sharp shake of the head. Presumably it wasn't in the kitchen. They'd have to find it soon. They'd been here an age already.

Then, at about half past three, Mr Caristan went upstairs. They heard him thumping round in the room above.

'Now!' Sara said, and she whipped open a cupboard,

rummaging quickly and thoroughly through the contents. Conor opened the sideboard drawers, feeling guilty. They worked quickly and in silence.

'No luck. Try the crates.'

There were a few of these still unpacked; they searched them hurriedly and even found a small gold box, but it was empty, and Conor thought it was too small anyway to be the one. There was nowhere else. On the dresser and the small tables the precious china glinted in the reddening light.

'It could be anywhere,' Conor muttered. 'Upstairs, in some suitcase . . .'

'Sshh. He's coming.'

When he came down, carrying some more books, she said, 'Mr Caristan, what would you say was the most important thing you've got? The most expensive, the most precious?'

He laughed. 'Ah well, the most important piece isn't necessarily the most expensive, Sara. But I keep my choicest delights in a cabinet upstairs. Come and see.'

Behind his back, she winked at Conor. As they climbed the stairs he thought how clever she was. He'd never have thought of that, or even known how to put it.

Caristan took them into the tiny front bedroom, with the window that looked across the Levels; miles of flat fields, lit now with the eerie western glow.

In the corner was an ornate walnut cabinet, with bowed legs. He unlocked the glass door with a tiny key.

'There we are. This is Sevres, and this is early Chelsea.'

'What about that?' Conor said, pointing with satisfaction to a small gilt-coloured box at the back.

'Oh that.' Mr Caristan chuckled, and lifted it out. 'Well, it's an example of what I was saying. It didn't cost much, but I like it. Local workmanship. Quite old too. Do you see here, the map of the estuary incised on the top? And the words look, AFON HAFREN, HEB DRUGAREDD . . . the river Severn, without mercy . . .'

'Can I see?' Conor said.

'By all means.' Mr Caristan dropped the box, surprisingly heavy, into his hands. 'Rather like a warning, isn't it?'

Sara crowded close. Conor could feel her excitement. He opened the lid, and a pang of sharp disappointment pierced him, until Caristan said, 'Now there's a secret drawer in that box, and I'll bet neither of you can open it.'

Of course, he'd forgotten! It must be the right box! He turned it, hurriedly, looking for a hidden catch, some knob.

'Oh let me,' Sara moaned, so he gave it to her.

'All right, clever. I suppose you'll find it.'

But she couldn't, and had to give it back at last. Conor shook the box and something rattled inside. Fighting his excitement he let his fingers explore the dull metal, and found a tiny crack. 'Got it!' He put his thumbnail in, and pushed. With a snap the drawer shot out. In it was a small gold ring.

'My mother's wedding ring,' Caristan said calmly. 'I keep it safe in there.'

Suddenly, frustration swept over Conor, a hot wave of anger and disappointment. He saw in an instant the cruelty of the long spell, the taunting green eyes of the woman in his dream, and hated them, hated the whole thing. His fingers clenched on the box.

'I'll bet,' he said, his voice oddly choked, 'that there was something more than a ring in there when you bought it.'

'Jewels? Precious stones?' Sara added, encouragingly.

Mr Caristan chuckled, fingering a china cup. 'Nothing so wonderful. Just a piece of old candle.'

At last! Conor thought. Sara's voice was wonderfully calm. 'I'll bet you were disappointed. What did you do with it?'

'Can't remember. Put it in a candlestick, I suppose.'

Sara flicked a look of worry, but Conor was staring past her shoulder with a grim face. She turned. On the windowsill was a vast assortment of candlesticks – some small round ones with handles, others tall and ceramic with painted flowers, or brass, in the shapes of dolphins and fish and birds. One or two looked like silver. Each had a white candle, all different sizes.

'Did you hear that?' Sara whirled and grabbed Caristan's arm, shooting Conor a swift, secret look. 'Downstairs. Someone's moving about! I heard them!'

'But the alarm . .!'

'Is it switched on?'

Caristan hesitated, as she knew he would.

'Come on then!' She pushed him towards the door; Conor heard them running hurriedly down the stairs.

Instantly he was at the windowsill, fumbling among the clutter of candlesticks, the countless white columns of wax. Which was it? How could he even tell? Downstairs a door slammed. Sara shouted something. He tugged a candle out, stared at it, stubbed it back in. Too small, surely. He tried another. It was so firmly jammed in its melted wax it took both hands to jerk out; a blue tin candlestick fell off the window with a clang. Was this it! He didn't even know!

And then he saw on the windowsill the end of a tiny red thread. He pounced on it, sweeping the rest aside, and tugged; a slim silver fish holding a small candle in its mouth juddered and fell over. In a flash he had the candle out and in his pocket, and was pushing the substitute in when Caristan announced 'False alarm' behind him.

'Was it?' Conor turned, his hands in his pockets. 'That's a bad pun, too.'

They both laughed, and Sara grinned behind them in the doorway.

As soon as they were down the lane and around the corner, she unclipped the lamp from the front of her bicycle. 'Right. Let's see it. Are you sure you got the right one?'

He brought it from his pocket. 'Sure enough. Remember what Meurig said about the thread?'

It was wrapped round the bottom third of the stub; a faded red thread pulled so tight that it had cut into the wax. Apart from that it was just as the fiddler had said, an ordinary kitchen candle, rather dirty yellowy-white, with a blackened wick.

They stared at it through the dimness.

'What did you think of my false alarm?' she said.

'Brilliant. I wouldn't have believed it for a second.'

She kicked him absently. 'It looks smaller than I'd thought. Do you think it's been burned?'

He shrugged, 'I don't know. Perhaps Meurig might.'

For a moment they thought of all those hours and minutes the flame might have licked away; then Conor closed his hand on it tight.

'Come on. I want to see his face when we give it back to him.'

The sun had gone; the sky was an eerie purple. From the west black clouds were mounting, and a fresh wind struck their faces as they climbed the steep steps to the top of the wall and stared at the sudden sheet of water.

The tide was full, immensely full, crashing against the wall! Spray whipped in great arches over their heads as the waves roared in and back, sucking with horrible cloops and gurgles through the stones. The river was a dark expanse, churning and boiling.

'Run!' Sara called, climbing on the bike. 'Quickly!'

She began to ride and he raced after her. Great drops fell on them; the sky hung heavy and low over their heads. Ahead the watchtower was a blaze of lighted windows but, as Conor glanced down, the path was a black thread and the raging tide crashed and bubbled and crashed just below him.

A shout came out of the darkness ahead; Sara answered, and waved. As she raised her arm the bicycle wobbled; one wheel slewed to the side, and suddenly she was down, Conor stumbling over her. He fell heavily, onto the wet mud, the breath thumped right out of him, wet grass against his face. Pain shot up one hand. He jerked off it, grabbing for the candle that slid and rolled down the slope. 'Sara!' he yelled, 'Sara! Get it!'

But the hand that picked it up was wet, with rings and bracelets of gold and weed; the hand of a woman with green eyes who was there for a moment, laughing, until she blurred and shimmered and dissolved into a great green wave that fell crashing over him, drenching him so that he flung his hand over his head and cowered. As the water ran down his neck and soaked his back he clenched his empty fist and yelled with anger. She had taken the candle!

He struggled up and squirmed to the edge but someone grabbed him and hauled him roughly back. 'Leave it!' Meurig shouted in his ear. 'Leave it! It's too late!'

8

'I broke two little bones in my hand.' Conor pulled
the stool up to the hearth. 'Not even enough for a
plaster. It's just strapped up.'

He knelt down and put a match to the newspaper
under the coals, touching it here and there with the
blue flame.

'Did you have an X-ray?' Sara asked, glancing at
the bandage.

'Yes. We had to wait ages. Went into town after.'
He shook the match out.

It had been nice to be in Newport with his mother,
and no Evan. He hadn't even minded trailing round
the shops.

'What about you?'

'Nice of you to ask,' Sara said drily. 'Cuts and
bruises. All over.'

He grinned; he could see one bruise shining on the
side of her face.

'Want a drink?' He crossed to the bar.

She swivelled. 'Gin and orange please, plenty of
ice.'

'Idiot. Is Coke all right?'

'I suppose I'll have to put up with it.'

As he was jerking the cap off the bottle his mother came in with a box and glanced at the fire. 'Oh that's better. That'll take the damp out of the air.' She came over and looked at Sara's bruise.

'Have you put anything on that?'

Sara went red. 'Butter. My nan swears by it.'

'So do I.' Mrs Jones tore open the box of crisps and pulled out two packets. She tossed them on the table. 'Presents. Is your bike still in one piece? Why you were out cycling in all that rain and wind I can't think. Conor will be out of rugby for weeks. What good is a winger who can't catch?'

'Thanks. It's all right – I mean the bike. The wheel was dented but my dad can straighten it.' Sara opened the crisps – salt and vinegar – and watched Conor bring one drink at a time, left-handed.

Evan came in and dumped the rest of the boxes on the counter.

'Eating all the stock I see,' he said, winking at her.

She smiled, briefly. He was bald at the front, his high forehead oddly shiny. She could see why Conor didn't like him.

He began to stack the boxes. 'And you know Conor, it's illegal for you to be served in here.' He came out from behind the bar and snorted with laughter. 'You'll get yourself banned, son.'

Conor glared.

'Oh don't tease him,' his mother laughed. 'Not now he's an invalid.'

They went out, giggling. Conor was silent with fury.

Sara crunched a crisp. 'Eat yours.'

'I don't want them. Those two are like a pair of schoolkids.'

'It must be nice living in a pub. Everything free.'

'It's only because you're here. Usually I have to pay.'

They were silent again. Then Conor said, 'I feel awful.'

'About Evan?'

'About Meurig.'

'Ah.' Sara crumpled the packet up and threw it onto the fire. It squirmed and melted into a burst of purple flame. 'So do I. He wheeled the bike home for me last night, after we'd brought you here, and he hardly said a word all the way. What a mess, Conor, after all our trouble! We had the candle in our hands! I can't believe it.'

'We'd better go and see him.' He wandered to the window and sat on the sill, looking out at the wall. 'You realize we've just made everything worse? I mean, she's got it now. She might do anything.'

Sara nodded, opening the other packet of crisps. 'Do you want these?'

'SARA!' he spun around.

'Oh all right, all right! I only asked. And she won't have burned it yet Conor. We won't find him dead, if that's what you're thinking. She's too canny.'

He hadn't thought of that. He was glad. It was a horrible thought.

A crowd of gulls was flapping and wheeling high above the watchtower. Conor looked up anxiously. 'There's no smoke. Do you think . .?'

'We'll soon see.' She thumped on the door; the sound echoed, a dull thud, around the stairwell inside. After a moment she pushed the door open and they went in.

'Meurig?'

Echoes hummed and dripped, but no one answered. They ran upstairs quickly and noisily, as if to keep the silence away.

The top room was dark; the grey clouds outside seemed so low that they pressed against the windows. Meurig was lying on his back on the bed, staring up at the cracked ceiling. He turned his head as they came in and sat up, slowly.

Sara shivered. 'It's freezing in here. Your fire's gone out.'

'Has it?' He looked absently at the cold ashes. 'I hadn't noticed.'

Conor sat down next to him. 'We came to say we were sorry about last night.'

'It wasn't your fault.' The fiddler leaned back against the wall, and ran his fingers through his ruffled hair. 'You did your part . . . but I should have realized that she'd know, that she would be waiting . . .' He shook his head and then looked at them, his face shadowed in the ominous light. 'When I saw you coming along the wall, I almost threw myself down those stairs but it was already too late. I saw her, for a moment, as she took it from you. You were lucky she didn't drown you.'

They were all silent. None of them wanted to think of what Hafren might do with the candle; what she might be doing at that moment. Conor thought of his dream; the dim flame burning in the drowned rooms and the floating weed.

'Can't we get it back?' he burst out.

'Don't be daft.' Sara was looking out of the window at the estuary. 'If she's got it it's out there somewhere, rolling around in all that water.'

Meurig gave her an odd look; Conor thought he was about to say something, but instead he dragged his coat from the end of the bed and pulled it on, and leaned back again.

'What sort of creature is she?' Conor asked.

'A water-spirit . . . I don't know. Some say a drowned princess, a force of nature. She's said to have an island, somewhere out there. Long ago the people of these parts would worship her, throw their gold and weapons to her, so that she wouldn't destroy their fields or steal their children. She remembers that; she's still hungry for it. Every river takes lives, but Hafren is the most treacherous. Three a year, man or beast. Remember the man in Chepstow, last week?'

They nodded. The man had been swept away; his body found miles upstream.

Meurig rubbed his face wearily with the back of one hand. 'She has me in her hands now. That scares me.'

Sara came over and pulled up a chair. 'You mustn't worry. Maybe Conor is right . . .'

Then she saw they were not listening to her. They were staring over her shoulder, and she turned and saw the sky grey and ominous, the sudden patter of rain.

'What is it?'

On the glass the rain moved wet fingers; they slid down, dragging, fumbling at the latch. Conor jumped up; his chair fell back with a smack, and at once the window crashed open; rain roared in on the gale. Mugs tipped and rolled, smashing on the floor. Ashes swirled up in a grey storm of spray, the sudden screaming of gulls.

Conor beat Meurig to the window, but it took both of them to force it shut. Meurig jammed the latch and wiped rain from his eyes. Then he turned, into a shocked silence.

Sara was staring at the opposite wall.

Running down it, in great brown letters that dripped to the floor, were the words:

OPEN THE SLUICES. LET ME IN.

After a moment Meurig crossed the room. They followed him, and knelt by the letters. Conor touched the O – it felt cold and gritty.

'What does it mean?' Sara said, her voice faint.

'What it says.' Meurig said. 'Letting her in. Letting the river on to the Levels. That's her price for the candle.'

'The sluices . . . you mean flood the reens?'

He nodded, and they stared in fear at the long, brown, running letters, now almost illegible. They both knew that the reens drained the low-lying land, and that excess water drained from them through sluices and gouts back into the river. If they were opened the river would run in, flooding the reens and overflowing, drowning fields and roads, running into houses, the pub, the church, and rising and rising until the Levels were a silver lake with trees and rooftops jutting through.

'You can't!' Sara muttered. 'It would mean a flood.'

He nodded. 'Exactly. That's what she wants.' He got up and stared out at the houses below. 'She wants me to betray all of them.'

9

After that, the weather got worse.

It rained all night; squalls of hard-driven spray that rattled against the windows. By morning the wind had risen to force 8, coming straight off the estuary.

Wiping the tables in the pub Conor lifted his head and saw a familiar yellow van rolling up the track, the words CALDICOT AND WENTLLWG LEVELS on its side half hidden by splashed mud. The driver came in whistling, a mass of glistening yellow oilskin. He nodded at Conor and went through to the back.

Thoughtfully, Conor drifted nearer, table by table. He caught snatches of talk through the open door.

'. . . an amber alert on the Wye, the Usk, and the Severn . . . it'll be on the lunchtime news . . . bridge down at Crick . . . road's awash, may be a burst main . . .'

Conor thought of Hafren. If those sluice-gates were open the whole of the Levels would be a drowned stillness at the next tide. But she had the candle. He flung the damp cloth into the sink angrily. If only he'd held on tighter.

Later, lunchtime customers began to arrive. The flood warning had got around.

'Tides are higher than they ought to be,' Goronwy Hughes said, lighting his cigarette with a spill from the fire. He looked over at Mr Caristan, hanging his coat up. 'You've got some sandbags, I hope?'

'Sandbags?' Mr Caristan looked at Conor. 'What for?'

'There's a flood alert. Only amber.'

'Ah,' Mr Caristan sat on a stool by the bar and ordered a whisky and soda from Evan. He smoothed his new silk waistcoat. 'That'll be way upriver, won't it? Minsterworth, Newbury . . . all those flat water meadows.' He sipped his drink. 'Now that's the kind of liquid I like.'

Evan laughed, leaning his broad arms on the bar. 'Quite right. And don't let them worry you mind. There'll be no flood here, not with the wall.'

'Perhaps it's the wall she hates most,' Conor muttered.

'Now by she,' Mr Caristan said, 'I suppose you mean the ancient personification of the river.' He winked at Evan. 'Sabrina fair, listen where thou art sitting . . . and all that.'

'I suppose I do,' Conor said sulkily.

'A poetic idea. Water as woman. The source of life . . . unpredictable.'

Evan laughed. 'They certainly are.'

At one o'clock Meurig came past the window and a moment later came in through the door. A few of the older men nodded at him. The fiddler looked worn, but determined; he grabbed Conor by the sleeve and drew him into a corner.

'Look,' he said. 'I've made up my mind. I've decided

to try and speak to her. It's dangerous . . . and probably quite useless, but it's the only thing I can do now. The weather's making things worse. There's an alert out.'

'I know.' Conor shook his head. 'How can you speak to her?'

'Call her. She'll come, if only to torment me. I can't do what she wants, Conor!'

'I know that. But I've been thinking. If she can flood the Levels – and they've flooded before, at least partly – then why does she need you?'

Meurig picked up a beer mat. 'To make it easier. Think about it. With the sluice-gates open the water level would rise slowly and silently. It would creep up. That's how she'd prefer it. No one would notice at first – there'd be no alerts, no warning – and then suddenly she'd catch them, all those people miles inland, the houses and farms and factories in Magor and Roget and Undy, where the people think they're safe. It would be a disaster! It would be the Great Flood all over again. Do you know how many died in that?'

'Over a hundred,' Conor muttered.

'Well it would be more this time.' Meurig looked at him anxiously. 'Will you come with me?'

Astonished, Conor glanced up. 'Of course I will. Sara too.'

A wan smile crossed the fiddler's face, but before he could say anything Conor's mother was there. 'Meurig,' she said. 'Look at you. You look half starved.'

'Do I?' He flipped the beer mat over in his long fingers.

'Come and have something to eat with us. No

62

arguing. I have money invested in you.' She marched off, her dark hair swinging.

'You'll have to come now,' Conor said. 'She won't take no.'

'I've already found that out!'

They ate in the kitchen – steak and kidney pie and chips – and despite his worry Meurig ate hungrily. He and Conor's mother chatted about music, and Conor grinned to himself to see Evan wandering back and forth through the kitchen for the slightest reason, giving them brooding looks. Jealous, was he? thought Conor, stabbing a chip with his fork. Good. Excellent.

It was nearly half past two before they got away to Ty Gwyn, half running the whole way into the rising gale. Already the ground was very wet; great pools filled all the ruts in the track and still the rain poured steadily down. Conor stamped his boot into a puddle. 'How much of this is her doing?'

Meurig shrugged, his eyes on the green, sodden fields. 'Who knows?'

'It won't be safe, calling her up.'

'If it worries you, Conor . . .'

Conor shook his head. 'Of course it worries me. Everything does. People are always telling me about it.' He stopped as he saw the fiddler's grin. 'And you needn't start either.'

Suddenly they were both laughing, the rain dripping from the ends of their hair. From the barn Sara watched them with astonishment.

'What's up with you?' she said, stepping aside to let them in.

Conor gasped for breath. 'Nothing.' He sat weakly on a bale of straw, and rubbed his side. 'Hysteria, I think.'

Sara looked at Meurig. 'I wouldn't have thought you had much to laugh about.'

'I haven't.' Serious, all at once, he said, 'We're going to speak to her.'

'You must be mad!'

'Yes,' he shrugged. 'Maybe I am. Maybe I've got no choice. Come if you want to.'

'Of course I want to!' She pulled on her hood and grinned at them. 'I'm not sure you two ought to be let out on your own!'

They left the farm by the back lane and ran over the wet fields. Meurig led them inland, over narrow bridges and down lanes, until Conor saw Marshall's reen in front of them, the wood on its far side. By now the rain had dwindled to a fine drizzle that hung in the air without even seeming to fall, blurring distances like mist. Water was everywhere around them, even here.

On the edge of the reen, Meurig stopped. 'This will do. She came here before.'

Sara dragged the soaking ends of hair from her cheek and looked around.

'How will you call her?'

'With this.' He unslung the bag from his back; took the fiddle out and began to tune it, quickly.

'What about the damp?'

'I'll manage. I'm used to damp.'

'Did they let you have it in prison?' Conor asked suddenly.

Meurig lifted his head. 'No,' he said quietly. 'They didn't.'

He put the fiddle under his chin and drew the bow

64

across it. A strange note shivered into the wet air; it lifted into an odd, lilting tune.

'What's that?' Sara said.

'It's a song a man heard once as he lay asleep on a faery hill. For ever afterwards, they say, he could never play anything else. This will bring her.'

Conor shivered. The music seemed to keen and cry in the dampness about him, like a live thing; he could almost imagine it to be the voice of something that drifted in the mist, out of sight. Meurig played slowly, ignoring the rain that ran down the bow and dripped from his fingers; he bent his head down and closed his eyes and the music slid out and hung softly and eerily over the marshland.

Conor watched the reen. The water lay still under its green cloth of algae. Broken stems of reeds pierced it; brown hollow stalks of last year's cow parsley and teazle, and a half rotten willow sprouted from the bank. Then, almost unnoticably, the surface trembled.

'Look,' he murmured.

Mist formed over the water; a low swirl of it drifted up. Underneath, far below the surface, a face was watching them. It blurred and moved with the rippling reen, its eyes watched them, green and narrow.

She rose, slowly, a creature of mist and water, and her hair and dress were never still; they ran and trickled, streaming with water and weed, the algae clothing her like heavy velvet. She sat on the bank opposite, watching Meurig, and Conor saw how her dress had no end, it just ran into the reen and was water. Gold glinted at her neck; through the mist he saw pearls in her slippery hair. The fiddler stared back at her. Slowly, he let the music die, lifting the bow and leaving only echoes in the murk.

For a moment no one spoke.

Then Hafren moved, turning her gaze on Conor. He stood still, cold. Before his eyes she blurred from hag to girl to woman, her sea-green gaze enfolding him like fear. Did she know about his dream? How could she?

Meurig came forward, the bow and fiddle hanging from his hands. He kept well clear of the water's edge.

'I can't do what you ask,' he said.

A low, choked hiss came out of the mist.

'Watchman, you will.'

Her voice was fluid and rippling; it was the cold bitter lap of the waves against a flat shore.

She spread her misty fingers out in the grass; water trickled from them into the reen. 'Or I will light the wick and melt your life away.'

Her eyes moved to Sara and Conor. 'You are his friends. Warn him.'

Conor cleared his throat. 'You don't understand . . .'

'Oh she does,' Sara said quietly. 'Of course she does.'

The woman flowed into a young girl, her voice bitter.

'It was my land. They took it away. Now I will take it back. Slowly.'

'And what about the people?' Meurig snapped.

Looking at him sideways, she dissolved away into mist. For a moment she was just a drift of vapour.

'Warn them.'

'It's impossible! There are hundreds of scattered farms, people's houses, livestock . . . we could never clear them all out . . . you know that!'

Her green eyes held his.

Suddenly Meurig crouched at the reen's edge, his fingers gripping the wet grass. His face was white and despairing. 'I can't do it! I can't! Nothing will make me!'

For a moment she watched him. Then, with one finger, she touched the smooth surface of the reen. The mat of tiny floating leaves opened, leaving a dark hole of water.

Conor edged closer. Far down, burning faintly, he saw the flame. It flickered, dwindling and rising, brilliant in the dark water.

Sara reached towards it, but Meurig grabbed her. 'Be careful! It's deeper than you think.'

The water at the reen's edge sent tiny, rippling fingers towards them.

'It's just out of reach,' Sara said.

Hafren watched them. 'It is far, far away,' she murmured. 'In my own safe place, beyond the borders of the world. I will not put it out. Second by second, you are dying.'

With an effort Meurig scrambled up and turned his back. He jammed the fiddle into its bag, his hands shaking. 'Come on,' he snarled. 'Let's go.'

'But Meurig, the candle . . .'

'LET HER BURN IT!' he yelled at them. 'She can't hurt me like that! I don't even believe it any more!'

But they knew he did.

The creature dwindled, moving down into the reen. Her hair spread on the surface; vapours rose about her, marsh smells and stale air; the green fetid smell of decay. 'Choose, Meurig,' she said.

He stood there, helpless, his eyes on the flame. Then all at once Sara shoved him aside. 'All right. We'll do what you want.'

'No!' Meurig rounded on her, but she took not the slightest notice of him. She knelt on the edge of the reen, her face close to the green eyes in the water. 'He's too upset; he doesn't know what he's saying, but we'll make sure he does it. When do you want the sluices open?'

The creature in the water slid nearer. She reached up a dripping hand and touched Sara's cheek. 'Tomorrow night,' she whispered. 'At the high tide; the moon and I will come together, hand in hand.'

'But you must put the candle out first.'

'Oh, my sweet . . .'

'You must!' Sara bent closer; Conor gripped her belt. 'You must. To give us time. And to show him it's worth it.'

Hafren moved away, into the reen. She looked down, and far below her the flame in the water went out.

'Tomorrow,' her voice rippled, bubbling from the green weed. 'Tomorrow you let me in. Or I burn his life away.'

10

Meurig sat with his head in his hands watching Sara pour the hot tea into three mugs, and stir it.

'Why did you say it?' he asked at last.

'Oh you're speaking to me now, are you? I said it to give us some time.' She brought the tea over, gave a cup to Conor and put Meurig's down on the table. He ignored it.

'But I can't do it!' he said wearily.

'I know that! We're not going to do it. But we are going to get that candle back.'

They both stared at her in astonishment. She sipped the tea and laughed. 'You look like two frogs in a pond.'

Conor frowned, but Meurig almost smiled, the first time for hours. He picked up the mug and stirred the tea. 'So tell us your great plan, Sara.'

'I haven't got one. I've done my bit, lying to that creature. Now it's your turn.' She sat on the bed and wriggled back against the wall, shuffling off her wellies and curling her legs up. 'And you should have the plan. You're the watchman.'

Meurig sipped his tea and gazed at the darkness outside the tower windows. 'Not much of one.' But he was thinking, they could see.

'Listen,' Conor said. 'Before, you said something about Hafren having an island out there . . .'

'So they say.'

'Out in the estuary?'

Meurig shrugged. 'You heard what she said. Beyond the borders of the world. It's her island. It's on no map, but sometimes seamen have seen it, a landmass where there should be none. Then the mist closes down and it's gone again. It's not a real island, not like Flatholm and Steepholm and Lundy. It's . . . somewhere else.'

Conor got up and looked out of the window, but it was too dark now; he could only see his own reflection, and a few lights, towards Weston.

'How can such things be?' Sara muttered, thinking of the title of a book she'd been reading.

'I don't know, How can we know? But there are tales of men who have been there . . . old stories . . .'

He drifted into thought. Conor looked at Sara. 'We'd need a boat.'

'There's Dad's. But he'd never let us. Not without him.'

'You can row.'

'Yes, but it's not that easy. There are the tides and sandbanks, shoals, currents . . . you know what the estuary is like . . .'

'It doesn't matter,' Meurig said quietly.

Sara glared at him. 'Of course it does! We're going to get that candle, so don't mope!'

He looked at her in surprise. 'Oh I'm not Sara, believe me. No, I mean the boat doesn't matter. I know where I can get someone to row me out, a way she won't feel us come.' He tapped the mug thoughtfully. 'But it will still be very dangerous. She could

70

easily drown us all. So I'm going to do this by myself –
I can't take the responsibility for you.'

'Meurig!'

'No.' He looked at them sadly. 'You've done
enough for me already. You found the candle.'

'And lost it again,' Conor muttered.

'That was her doing. I can't bring you into this, not
now. And that's the end of it, Conor. No arguing.'

And for all their nagging and asking, that was all
he would say. But later, as they were leaving, Meurig
pressed something cold and small into Conor's hand.
'Keep it safe,' he said in a low voice. 'It's the key to
this tower. There always has to be a watchman,
Conor. No matter what happens.'

He led them out into the rain, kissed Sara gently
and ruffled Conor's hair.

'I'll be back, don't worry.' He looked up at the
clouds, driving in over the dull sky. 'But remember,
tomorrow is the highest tide. And she'll be coming.'

Conor and Sara walked silently along the wall, the
wind buffeting against them. Neither wanted to speak,
and they couldn't in any case, not with the wind
snatching away every breath. Out in the river the tide
moved with a turgid roar, spreading white foam on
the mud, closer with each wave.

When they came to the concrete steps they climbed
down carefully and stood in the shelter of the wall.
Out of the wind it felt warmer; Sara rubbed her ears
and said, 'He's not doing this without us, whatever
he says.'

Conor grinned. 'I knew you'd say that.'

'We'll follow him,' she decided. 'I'll come to the

71

pub early; we can watch the tower – he'll have to walk along the wall, and we'll see him. He'll lead us to this boat.'

'What then?'

Sara shrugged and began to walk, avoiding the nettles. 'We go with him. We'll make him take us.'

Conor nodded and then stopped suddenly in the path. 'Oh hell!' he hissed.

'What?'

'Tomorrow! It's my mother's birthday – we were going to the pictures.'

She went back to him. 'What are you going to do?'

'I don't know.' Feeling the rain he walked on, but at the gate to the farm they stopped again, and Conor picked absently at the ivy, pulling a leaf off and shredding it. 'I'll have to come with you,' he said at last. 'Trouble is, it means Evan will have to take her . . .'

'Right, I'll see you tomorrow,' Sara waved and began to run up the lane. 'And stop worrying about him. This is more important.'

Conor turned away. 'I wish I could,' he muttered.

At eleven next morning they sat in the window of Conor's bedroom, watching the dark line of the wall against the sky. Behind them, the radio spoke to their backs.

'. . . Meanwhile flood alerts on six rivers in South Wales have been increased to red; on the Wye at Tintern, the Usk, the Afon Llwyd, the Trothi, Ebbw and Severn, both at Brecon and downstream. The recent heavy rain is pouring down from the hills and a spokesman from the rivers authority warned today that coastal defences are on full alert for tonight's high tides . . .'

'They'd better be,' Conor muttered.

'Rising gales from the west and the recent strange tidal surges in the Severn estuary have added to the danger. Sandbags are being issued and the army and coastguard are standing by. Now, attention all shipping . . .'

Sara grabbed his sleeve. 'There he is!'

Meurig had come out of the tower and was standing up on the wall, his hands in his pockets. They could see the slight bulge of the fiddlebag as it hung over his shoulder.

'What's he waiting for?'

'I don't know!' Sara snapped. 'Let's get outside, quick.'

They raced down the stairs, swept past Conor's mother and out of the door. Then, hesitantly, Conor came back.

'Have a nice time,' he muttered.

'Thanks. Are you sure you won't change your mind?'

He kicked the step. 'I can't.'

'Well, don't look like that. It's not the end of the world.' She smiled at him. 'I don't mind going with Evan, you know.'

Conor turned his head. 'That's good then, isn't it.' He went out, quickly. 'See you later.'

Sara was waiting impatiently. 'Come ON!'

He swept past her, hardly listening. They ran to the edge of the track, but the top of the wall was empty. They scrambled up, looking anxiously into the wind, but the shore was a blank expanse of purple-grey mud. Then they saw him. He was picking his way carefully along the foot of the wall, leaping from stone to stone, keeping to the solid patches of shingle and weed.

'Get down.' Conor pushed Sara back over the side of the grassy bank and slid down beside her. 'He's keeping out of sight – he must have guessed we'd be watching. See?'

Meurig had turned and glanced back; apparently reassured, he hurried on.

'We'll have to keep to this side of the wall,' Sara muttered. 'Come on.'

It was difficult, scrambling along the steep wet bank of grass, and having to keep checking too, that the fiddler was still ahead of them. After a while he scrambled over the treacherous foreshore and up onto the rocks; he climbed to the top of the wall and then over it, down the grassy slope on their side. Safe behind a willow, they watched him.

Meurig crossed two fields, jumping the reens. It was hard to follow without him seeing, and once Conor put his foot into the water with a sickening splash, but a light mist was closing around them, and that helped.

The fiddler kept east, heading towards the Porton grounds. Then he turned down a dank track back towards the estuary.

Conor and Sara stopped to draw breath.

'Where's he going?'

Sara opened the gate and let Conor through. 'I don't want to worry you Conor, but this leads to Ferryman's Pill.'

'Isn't that supposed to be haunted?'

'So they say.'

He looked at her, and at the dim track ahead, winding into mist. Dark trees twisted at each side, their boughs contorted by the sea-wind. Far ahead, the fiddler's shadow had flickered out of sight. Reluctantly, they followed.

'What does he want down here?' Conor muttered.

The mist seemed to swallow sound. The cries of gulls died away; the coughs of cows faded behind them. Down here it was silent, and dank. Water dripped without sound from black branches.

Quickly, their feet crunching slightly on the stony track, Conor and Sara followed the fiddler's shadow. Ferryman's Pill was a tiny inlet of the river, a place where mist always hung, where strange blue lights were sometimes seen at night. Marsh gas, people said, but others spoke of haunting, a grey shape that moved into the darkness. Whatever it was, Conor thought grimly, he'd rather not know. What did Meurig want with this place?

Sara caught his arm. Ahead, a shadow in the mist, they saw Meurig was climbing the wall. The wall was lower here, not so strong. As soon as he was over they scrambled up between the bushes, disturbing a heron that rose and flapped over the trees.

'Can you see him?' Sara peered over the top, her hands in the mud.

'I can't see anything,' Conor whispered.

A grey wall of mist confronted them. The tide was coming in; it had almost filled the narrow pill and was lapping the mud, but they could see nothing out there. Then, as if he had materialized out of nowhere, Conor saw Meurig. He was standing on the spit of shingle, waiting. Fog wrapped him, so that sometimes they barely saw him, and then his figure was clear, his fixed gaze staring out at nothingness.

'Move up,' Sara muttered.

Conor wriggled forward, lost his footing, and slid, with all his weight on his hands. The sudden pain of the fracture made him gasp; a half stifled expulsion of breath that hissed in the silence.

Meurig turned like a cat.

Teeth clenched, Conor waited, letting the pain ebb. Sara glared at him.

'Get up from there!' the fiddler said at last. 'Conor!'

With a bitter look at each other they stood up on the wall.

'Go back!' Meurig hissed. 'Now! While there's time!'

'We can't . .'

'You must!' He took a step towards them. 'Sara, go back!'

It was too late. Over his shoulder they could already see the shape moving in the mist. Drifting without a sound, like a shadow, it glided in towards the shore; a grey boat, frail as a cobweb, glinting with damp. And Conor's heart clenched as he saw the man who rowed it; an old man, his hair grey as the mist; a man who looked up and watched them, dripping with water, his face like one of the drowned.

11

For a moment no one moved. Then Meurig said, 'Come over here' without even looking at them. As they scrambled hastily down the rocks Conor stared at the figure in the boat; it watched him, unmoving.

When they were beside him the fiddler muttered, 'You're a pair of fools. Don't say anything. Leave the talking to me.'

Raising his voice he spoke to the image in the mist. 'We need to go to Hafren's island. Do you know the way to that place?'

The old man gazed back. Conor was almost sure he had not heard. It was hard to see where the grey rags he wore ended and the mist began; he seemed to fade and shimmer like an illusion of the fog.

Meurig moved forward, balanced on the sunken stones. 'Will you take us?' he said urgently. 'I'm the watchman; these are my friends. We need your help against the malice of the river. We need to be secret . . . only you can do that.'

For a moment a change came into the ferryman's eyes – his gaze moved to Conor and Sara, a quick scrutiny that made them both shiver, as if at the touch of something damp. Then he took one frail hand from the oars and beckoned.

Meurig hesitated. Then he turned. 'Come on.'

He led them over the stones, their feet slithering into the liquid mud; he climbed carefully into the boat and Sara followed, sitting beside him. Conor stepped in awkwardly, feeling the craft give and sway beneath his weight. He sat, quickly.

Now the old man was very close to them, but still indistinct, as if he might fade to nothing. Sea water dripped from his hair; his clothes were strewn with bladderwrack and tiny fronds of lichen. The boat itself was a grey cobweb, its timbers swollen and encrusted with barnacles, cracked and gashed and in places transparent. A crab scuttled through the water that washed at Conor's feet. It smelt rotten and it was. He bent forward.

'Meurig . . .'

'Quiet Conor. I warned you not to come.'

Meurig had taken something out of his pocket; he held it out and ferryman looked at it. Then slowly, he put out one grey hand, and Meurig dropped the silver coin into his palm. For one fascinated moment Conor thought it would go right through, but the vague fingers closed about it. The ferryman put the coin into some fold of his clothes. Then he took the oars and prodded the boat off the mud bank; when it was free he sat back and began to row, with long, sweeping strokes, his wet hands tight on the wood, his face, with its remote gaze, fixed on his passengers.

Conor looked away from the drowned eyes, but the boat was moving in a solid greyness; he could see the oars dipping into the dark choppy water, but beyond that, nothing. He realized how quiet it had become.

Even the foghorn sounding at Nash Point had faded out; apart from the creak of the rowlocks all sound was lost. They could have been anywhere.

Sara gave him a lop-sided smile over her shoulder.

'I'm all right,' he muttered. Then he said 'Meurig . . . won't she know?'

Meurig stared out into the fog. 'Can even Hafren feel the drift of a ghost on her back? I don't know Conor. It was all I could think of.'

Conor looked past him. What was stopping the ferryman drowning them all, he wondered. How did the drowned feel about the living . . . did they feel, were they even there? Why did he still haunt the river? He longed to ask, but dared not.

The ferryman pulled the oars, rhythmically, as if he had no thoughts or feelings, and the motion of the boat became stronger; they swirled and drifted in new cross-currents; the prow lifted and fell with increasing depth. Conor started to feel very seasick. He gripped his hands tight together, feeling the saliva gather, the sweat start down his back. Oh don't let me be sick, he thought grimly. Not now.

Fog swirled about them, cold and clammy. Once a gull screamed and another answered. Water slapped against the sides of the boat. He thought about his mother and Evan in the cinema, about Hafren and the candle. He felt dizzy and was shivering, his teeth gritted tight. He felt Meurig scramble back and sit next to him, put a firm arm round him.

'Hang on Conor.'

Miserable and ashamed Conor muttered, 'I'm all right. I'm all right.' And then, to his dim surprise, he realized the swaying had stopped.

The boat seemed to have entered suddenly onto

some still sea, barely a ripple passing under it. As the ferryman rowed them on the mist began to fade, drifting in thin snatches around them, breaking up, until with magical abruptness they were in sunlight, on smooth blue water, crowds of kittiwakes flapping and calling above them.

Conor wiped his face with his hand.

'Better?' Meurig asked.

'Great. Ready to run a marathon.'

Sara grinned. 'Where are we?'

They were nowhere. Both banks of the wide river had gone; they were floating in an endless expanse of water, and there before them was an island, its tall gashed cliffs white with screaming birds.

In the sunlight the ferryman and the boat were incredibly faint; Conor could almost see the waves through the planks that he gripped so hard. But the knot in his stomach was loosening; he raised his head cautiously, and felt the salt sting of the wind freshen his face.

They were under the island now, and the cliffs stood high above them. At any other time he would have been amazed and delighted with the birds – gannets and razorbills and kittiwakes, even puffins, wheeling and screeching and flashing into the water – but now he only cared about landing.

The ferryman guided his craft carefully along the foot of the cliffs, among the swirling eddies, and then, rounding some rocks, they saw a small stretch of shingle, with the waves washing in.

With a sweep of the oars, the ferryman drew them in, and the keel of the boat grated hard on the beach.

Meurig climbed out, knee-deep in the clear water. He helped Sara over the side, and then Conor followed, still shaky, but shrugging off Sara's hand. She grinned at him. 'All right, hero, have it your own way.'

Meurig leaned on the gunwale. 'Thank you.'

The old man watched him, and then stretched across. His ghostly fingers caught the fiddler's sleeve, and he spoke, with a voice like a whisper of frost, hoarse and long unused.

'You have paid. I will wait for you.'

Meurig nodded. 'Where?'

'Where you are.'

They waded ashore and out onto the shingle. Sara tried to wring out the ends of her trousers.

'You'll have to take them off for that,' Conor muttered.

'No chance, son.'

He looked up at Meurig, and then out to where the boat was, but the ferryman and his craft were gone; before them the sea was unbroken to the far horizon.

'I thought he said . . .'

'He did. And he is, somewhere.' Meurig turned, easing the fiddle on his back. 'Come on. Let's see where we are.'

The beach was tiny, smelling of fish and seaweed and bird droppings. At the back a thin path led up the cliff, broken and dangerous, but there, as if it had been used before. They climbed up; Meurig first, then Sara, and finally Conor, who insisted on coming last. He still felt that he'd made a fool of himself in the boat, though neither of the others had said anything. He felt better now, and drew in deep breaths of the salt air.

The path was slippery; they had to hold onto the wet rocks. Birds shrieked about their heads; their gaping throats red, beaks wide.

Sara ducked. 'They're attacking us!'

'They're not. They're just interested,' Conor said.

Meurig glanced down. 'Keep quiet. We don't know what's at the top.'

But when they got there, they found there was nothing but grass; tussocky, rough grass studded here and there with thin gorse bushes, their flowers brilliant yellow against the sky.

'Where is this island?' Sara muttered, picking a sprig of thrift and pushing it into her jumper.

Meurig stared over the waving grass. 'It's nowhere in our world.' He turned to them. 'I don't know what might happen here, even who is here, and whether they know about us. We have to get the candle and be back before the tide.'

Sara nodded, tucking her hair behind her ear.

'Where do we look?' Conor asked.

'This way.' The fiddler turned and began to walk into the wind. 'It seems as good as any.'

They walked across the island to a low hill that reared up before them, dotted with white boulders. When they reached the top they crouched out of the wind.

On the other side the island was just as bare; waving grass, and beyond that, dunes and shingle, the long waves washing in, the birds scattered on the shoreline among stones and pebbles.

Conor put both fists on the grass and leaned his chin on them. 'It's empty.'

'No,' Meurig said, his eyes searching the scene. 'It can't be.'

'But we can see all the island from here, more or less. It's not very big.'

'And it's not empty.' The wind whipped the fiddler's dark hair over his eyes and he brushed it aside. 'Look. Down there. That rock by the stunted tree . . .'

Conor gazed down at the shore. He squinted, and then opened his eyes in surprise. 'It's a cat!'

'Hush!' Meurig pulled him down at once.

The white cat sat on a rock, licking its paw. As if it had heard it lifted its head for a long moment, and looked up the hill towards them. Then it carried on washing.

Sara let out a soft breath. 'Is it hers?'

'I wouldn't be surprised.' Meurig eased a cramped knee. 'We shouldn't let it see us; luckily the wind is blowing towards us. Back off, back down the hill.'

At the bottom they sat in a hollow behind some bushes.

'A cat can't hurt us,' Sara said.

No one answered. They all knew the cat was a threat, somehow.

'The candle is here,' Meurig muttered, his arms around one knee. 'I know it is. I can feel it, close . . .'

'Then we'll have to try going round,' Sara said, 'along the shore.'

'What about the cat?'

'Hope for the best.'

Meurig gave her a wry smile. 'I'm not very good at that.'

'I'd noticed.' She pulled him up. 'But I am.'

They explored the edges of the island. Most of it was cliff, apart from the small beach they'd landed at, but when they had worked their way round to the other side they saw it was flatter, with dunes of soft yellow sand, marram and thrift growing through it. It slid under their feet, and they left great hollow footprints down the slopes. At the bottom of one Sara stopped and emptied the sand from her shoes.

'It's not going to be here,' Conor muttered to her.

'He seems to think so.'

'But he wants it so badly. He may be fooling himself.'

She stood up, and put her shoe on, balancing with one hand on his shoulder. 'It doesn't matter. We've got to do what we can.'

Meurig was already walking out onto the wet beach towards the cliffs at one end; they ran after him quickly, climbing over the tumbled boulders, their feet slithering over barnacles and limpets. In all the rock pools were tiny yellow and brown cockles, and crabs that scuttled away and buried themselves, and once or twice Conor saw things that flicked out of vision; strange fish and eels that quivered and gleamed. Then he climbed up the cracked sides of a great tilted slab of stone, and saw the cave.

It opened in the hill side like a mouth; black and silent. Below him, Sara was sitting on a rock, looking at it, Meurig beside her, his face pale.

Damp air breathed out from the cave; the tidewater ran right up into it, knocking the walls and slooping into pools with strange echoes; rolling the rattling heaps of stones.

Conor scrambled down. 'In there?'

The fiddler sucked a cut finger. 'There's nowhere else. They say the gate of the underworld is a cave like this.'

'Don't be so encouraging,' Sara laughed. 'Come on, Meurig, it'll be all right.'

A rattle of stones made them look up. 'Will it?' he muttered.

From the top of the cliff the small cat was looking down at them, its ears flat.

12

Almost as soon as they saw it, the cat was gone.

'It's coming!' Conor said, but Meurig and Sara were already scrambling into the cave. He dropped down and raced after them.

They slid and slipped on the banks of wet pebbles; the noise made Conor wince. 'It'll hear us,' he muttered; his voice ringing in the darkness above.

'Let it!' Sara's feet splattered the pods of bladderwrack. 'It saw us anyway. Oh come on, Conor!'

The cave stank of fish. Water dripped and plopped around them, and the walls narrowed as they went further in until they could only just see the smooth rock, glistening green and purple, oiled and worn by the tide. The roof was low here. After only a few minutes they reached the back and Conor thought they were trapped. Then, in the shaft of daylight, he saw the hole.

It was a tiny doorway, no more than three feet high. It was made of three great slabs set in the wall, one lintel on top of two uprights. He crouched and gazed at them, and saw, with a peculiar shiver, that they were carved with spirals and crude waving lines, like children used to draw water.

In the hole was black emptiness. The air from it felt cold and damp.

Sara crouched beside him. 'In there?' She twisted round to look up at Meurig. 'We'll have to crawl!'

He nodded.

A click of sound made them all turn, but the cave mouth was an empty blue, screaming with birds.

'Something's upset them.'

Meurig crouched, 'I'll come last.'

'Have we got any light?' Conor murmured.

'A few matches, but we'll save those. Go on Sara.'

And she went, quickly, on hands and knees, under the lintel. Conor followed, folding himself up. He had to keep his head low, but even as he crawled through the tiny entrance the roof of the tunnel scraped against his back. In front of him, the soles of Sara's boots scuffled into blackness.

'It's too low,' he muttered, hearing Meurig struggle behind him.

'And it doesn't get any higher,' Sara's voice came back, muffled and annoyed.

They crawled deep into the cliff, down the tiny tunnel. Conor's knees quickly became sore; his palms were pitted and scuffed with the sandy grit; his right hand ached in its dirty bandage. Sometimes he could feel that the floor was smooth, paved with slabs of rock, and he thought the walls widened a little, but then it all closed in again, until at last he could feel rock on each side of him, pressing against him. A wave of panic almost overcame him. Sara in front, Meurig behind, blocking the air, and none of them could possibly turn around . . . what if he got stuck there, in that airless hole? He told himself not to be stupid. He could breathe. It wasn't stuffy. That was

86

imagination. He'd made a fool of himself in the boat and it wasn't going to happen again.

Then he stopped, resting his raw palms, and listened.

'Sara! Wait!'

Ahead of him the shuffles stopped. Her whisper came back, irritably.

'What?'

'It's Meurig. I can't hear him.'

Conor lay down on one elbow and twisted his head awkwardly. A light shower of dust fell into his eyes; he rubbed them and hissed 'Meurig! Are you stuck?'

Something shifted in the darkness a long way back. 'Not quite,' the fiddler gasped. 'I'm thin enough. Does it get any wider up there?'

Conor rubbed at his eyes. 'No. Are you sure we should go on?'

Meurig wriggled up behind him. 'I can't see how we can go back! And I know it's here. Believe me.' He bumped against Conor's foot. 'Is that you? Go on, quickly.'

Conor sighed and squirmed forward. 'I've heard of being in a tight spot,' he muttered, 'but never this tight.'

Somewhere ahead, Sara giggled. Then she said 'Hey! It's getting wider. Oh the relief! It's getting . . . Oh Conor, look!'

He put his elbows down and hurried. 'What?'

But with a rattle and a slither she was gone, and light glimmered through a small hole in front of him.

'We're coming out,' he called back to Meurig, and then squirmed through the hole after her, spilling hands first onto a soft cold bank of sand.

He drew his knees up under him, and gazed around

the cave. It was immense; a shadowy cavern high as a cathedral; its roof lost in the darkness. A peculiar light glimmered around him; a greenish, phosphorescent shimmer that rippled over stalactites, twisted formations of rock, pillars of quartz and salts mirrored in hundreds of pools of clear water. It was a chamber of mirrors and crystals, cold and secret, utterly silent.

Meurig rolled out and flexed his arms, painfully. Then he pulled the fiddle out from under his coat and slung it on his back.

They scrambled up the bank to Sara. The light confused them, played tricks with them. Gradually, they saw that the cave was not one, but a labyrinth, and behind pillars and columns, and through holes in the rock the pools reflected each other endlessly. There were banks of shattered quartz, and great curtains and solid waterfalls of stalactites, glistening white and smooth, melting and folding into each other through slow centuries of infinitesimal growth.

Sara raised an eyebrow at Meurig. 'Still sure?'

'Certain.'

His voice murmured oddly in hollow places; it came back whispering at them from unexpected corners. Drops fell into several pools, as if the vibrations had disturbed them. Conor felt that no one had ever spoken here before.

'Well,' Sara muttered, 'let's find it. That cat can't be far away.' Meurig didn't answer; Conor saw how tense he was. With a rattle of stones he climbed over the floor of the cave and the others followed. The ground was broken and shattered; the air cold. The strange light made them feel they were underwater.

The fiddler made his way over the rocks to the

margin of the nearest pool; he bent over it, and as Conor came from behind he saw Meurig mirrored perfectly in the dark, clear water. 'Look,' the fiddler said, with a peculiar satisfaction in his voice. 'Her treasure house.'

And he touched the water.

Instantly, all reflections broke. Conor saw, deep in the pool, hundreds of skulls, littered on the pale sand; thousands of them, a floor of lost faces, white as ivory. Lying between them were coins, scatterings of jewellery, gold rings, torques, great necklaces of rubies. The more he looked the more he saw. Swords, some with their blades broken; silver armrings; tiny carved wooden figures all warped and unrecognizable, swollen by the sea. There were shields half buried in the sand, tarred rope, even a child's doll with one arm gone, lying on its side, smiling. Deep in the dark corners were strange, inexplicable objects; antlers and pebbles knotted together, crude stone figures of women, a piece of yellow oilskin, quite modern.

'What is all this?' Sara asked quietly.

Meurig pulled up his sleeve and plunged his arm in deep, groping for something within reach of his fingers. He touched a wooden figure and pulled it out, dripping.

'I told you – her treasures. Look at this.'

The wood was seamed and split; the figure was a woman, its long hair marked with crude slashes; a fish carved across it.

'Is it her? Hafren?'

'I would think so. An offering, probably, thrown to the river centuries ago. She's brought them here, all the sweepings of the tide.' He nodded down at the rippling pool. 'Some of it – those antlers, look, those marked stones, could have been here for thousands of years.'

Conor watched a shoal of tiny fish swim through an open jaw.

'What about the skulls?'

'They didn't just throw in objects,' Meurig said darkly. He dropped the votive figure; they watched it float slowly down. 'Men have sacrificed to the river since before Stonehenge was built – to keep her back from the fields, to stop her drowning their cattle and their children.'

They were silent. Then Sara gripped Meurig's arm. 'Look,' she said, her voice choked.

'What?'

'There! Oh there, look, by that box! Can't you see it!'

Meurig grabbed the rock and hung out over the pool.

'Oh God, Sara!'

Then Conor saw it too. It was a tiny white cylinder of wax, half buried in the sand. A filament of red thread wound about it hung still in the water.

His heart thumped. 'The candle! Meurig . . .'

But Meurig was already swinging the fiddle from his back.

'No!' Conor said quickly. 'Let me get it!'

Meurig stared. 'Why you?'

'No reason.' Conor already had his coat and shoes off; he tugged his pullover over his head. 'Except that I lost it, so I should get it back. And the pool is very deep.'

'Conor's a good diver,' Sara explained, 'and he's got a life-saving award.'

Meurig hesitated. 'I don't know.'

'I'm going!' Conor felt he had to go. He'd been useless in that stupid boat and neither of them had said anything. If it had been Sara he knew he'd have made fun of her.

Meurig shrugged. 'All right. Be careful.'

Conor laughed. 'Don't worry.' He drew the cold, salty air deep into his lungs, put his head down, and dived.

The water was icy; it gripped him tight. Down and down he went, kicking deeper, feeling the pressure build against his nostrils and eyes and chest. Fish scattered under his hands; bubbles broke and blurred the floor of skulls, the peculiar twisted pieces of wood, the doll grinning at him. And there was the candle; his reaching fingers grasped it, scooped it out of the cold sand that lifted and clouded the water like smoke. He put his feet among the bones and pushed up, feeling the silent weight inside him swell, the pain in his ears and chest pound. Light rushed towards him; air and sound exploded into his lungs.

'Brilliant!' Sara was shouting. 'You've got it!'

He swam to the rocks and hauled himself wearily out of the water. Meurig helped him out, and Conor gave him the candle, without a word. The fiddler's long fingers closed about it, tight.

'It's not much smaller,' Sara said quietly, after a while, but Conor thought that at least a centimetre had gone, and from Meurig's shake of the head the fiddler thought so too.

Shivering, Conor picked up his shirt and flung it on, his fingers fumbling with the buttons. On the third one, he froze.

In the shadows on the far side of the cave, a stone had rattled.

They turned silently, hardly breathing, three shadows among the rocks. The entrance to the tunnel was a black gash, barely visible.

Another pebble clicked. Meurig stiffened, and touched Conor's shoulder. He nodded. He had already seen it. On the wall, moving eerily in the green underwater light, the immense shadow of the cat slipped from darkness to darkness.

13

At once, soundlessly, Meurig unthreaded his cloth bag and pulled out the fiddle, his eyes never leaving the stealthy movement on the wall. The shadow paused; they saw the cat's head turn slightly, its tongue flicker.

Meurig glanced at Conor, and gave a curt jerk of his head. They backed, foot by foot, silently from the water, until Sara sent a scatter of stones sliding and rattling. She pulled a face of disgust. 'Sorry.'

'Doesn't matter. It can smell us anyway.'

With the faintest click of pebbles, the cat had come round a pillar of rock. Since they had seen it outside it had grown, impossibly. Its white fur bristled; water beads glinted and rolled down its back. Two intelligent amber eyes watched them. Lightly, the huge cat leapt up onto a rock and crouched down, spitting and growling in its throat. It was about five feet away from them.

No one dared move. Conor was shivering with cold; he clamped his arms tight around him.

'Now what?' Sara said, barely opening her lips.

Meurig lifted the bow. Then he stood stock-still. The cat was preparing to spring. Its ears went suddenly flat; its pupils narrowed, its tail thrashed from side to side. Its gaze was fixed on Conor.

'Move!' Meurig yelled, pushing him aside. But even as Conor heard, the cat leapt. It landed with a heavy thump on his chest, knocking him flat, a spitting, scratching fury. He gasped, tried to heave it off, its breath stinking of fish, its spread claws slashing the skin under his ear. Warm blood ran down his neck.

Then the cat was gone; whirling with a snarl of rage on Sara, who turned and ran, leaping up a pile of unstable scree to a narrow ledge, the cat racing after her, silent. She flung a stone at it, just missing, and it stopped, tail swinging wildly. Conor staggered up.

'Here,' Meurig snapped. He was in a cleft in some rocks; Conor raced across and threw himself in behind.

'All right?'

'I think so. It was so quick!' He held a tissue to his neck; it reddened instantly.

'Use this.' Meurig gave him a handkerchief. 'Is it deep?'

'No, but it stings . . . What are you doing?'

'Something useless, maybe.' He stopped tuning and raised the fiddle to his chin.

'Meurig,' Sara warned. 'It's coming after you.'

The cat had turned from her; dodging another stone it prowled towards Meurig, its eyes glinting like glass in the green light.

Wedging himself in the cleft Meurig put the bow across the strings. 'Cover your ears,' he said.

'What?'

'Do it! You too, Sara!'

Slowly, he dragged the bow across the strings. A

94

sound broke from the fiddle, a soft, unnatural hum, so quiet it was almost unheard, but the echoes in the cave took it and murmured it over and over. Water trembled. Drops fell into pools.

Conor felt quite strange; he put his hands to his ears quickly and watched the cat. It blinked, but stayed quite still, watching the fiddler intently. Meurig let the note drift off into silence. Then he played another; exquisitely low and soft, a long, long, languid sound.

The cat answered. Deep in its throat it made a snarl.

Half-smiling, Meurig began to play.

The music was uncanny, if it even was music. At first it seemed just a loose gathering of sounds; strange, slow notes, long and winding, humming round the cave so that echo and music merged. Conor found he could not keep his attention on the sounds; his thoughts kept sliding away, into a looming darkness and weariness, a tiredness in his arms and legs and head.

When he looked at Meurig again, he knew with a dull shock that some time had passed. The cat was sitting now, its tail out straight behind it, its eyes intelligent slits, unblinking.

Across the cave he saw Sara sitting on the ledge, feet dangling. Her eyes were empty, her arms loose in her lap.

Still the fiddle played; faint, drifting, increasingly sleepy sounds that echoed endlessly in the still green silence, until Conor felt that the cave was heavy with sound, that even the drip of water into pools slowed, became an unhurried descent of thick globules, wobbling slightly, falling into silvery metallic fluid that opened to receive them soundlessly. And blurring with the music another murmur hung in the cave; a rich, satisfying purr, drifting into warm darkness, into the comfort of fur . . .

'Conor.'

Someone had hold of him; was shaking him.

'Conor.'

Wearily, he opened his eyes. A cold hand clamped over his mouth; he squirmed.

'No sound,' Meurig breathed. 'Not a whisper. Understand?'

Dizzy, he nodded.

The fiddler stepped back and moved aside, and Conor saw the cat. It was lying curled up, fast asleep, its tail coiled tight around it; a white, barely stirring heap of fur.

He breathed deeply, trying to clear his head. He felt muzzy and dazed; his eyes were tired and it was difficult to focus. Meurig was talking to Sara quietly; he helped her down from the ledge and beckoned to Conor; he went over, lifting his feet carefully between the rubble on the floor.

'What did you do?' Conor breathed. 'I'm half asleep!'

Meurig smiled briefly. 'Something I learned. Your collar is soaked – has the bleeding stopped?'

Conor felt the handkerchief he had jammed against his neck. 'I think so. Everything seemed to stop.'

'Right.' Meurig gazed over at the cat. 'Now make no sound, none. It could easily wake up. Let's get back up that passage, quickly!'

They crept around the rocks and past the treasure-filled pools, glimpsing their own anxious, dirty faces upside down in the clear water. The cave seemed bitterly cold now, and Conor still shivered from his dive; his wet clothes clung to him uncomfortably. Once he stumbled, and grabbed a frail hanging needle of stone; it snapped with a loud crack that echoed high in the roof. They stood in terror, staring back. The cat did not get up; they could just see it, a pale smudge in the rippling green light.

At last Sara managed a wan smile. 'Next time fall over, Conor. It'll make less noise.'

'Don't worry, I'll have died of hypothermia before then.'

She grinned, and followed Meurig, but the fiddler was blocking the way.

'Come on Meurig, move.'

He stepped aside, silent.

'Oh hellfire!' Sara gasped.

Before them, the cave was flooding with a great pool of black water, lapping at their feet, rising almost visibly up the green-stained wall of the cave. Under its surface, full to the roof, they could see the tiny dark entrance to the tunnel.

Conor groaned, feeling dismay soak him like the damp through his clothes. Meurig sat down on a rock, cradling the fiddle gently. He looked distraught, almost afraid.

'The tide,' he said numbly. 'Oh God, I'd forgotten the tide!'

Sara and Conor looked at each other.

'We're trapped,' she said, after a moment.

'Looks like it.' Conor sat by the fiddler. Each of them was thinking the same thing; of the great tide surging up the river under the moon, the powerful brown muscles of the river shouldering against the land.

'Well it won't do,' Sara said quickly. 'We can't just sit here and drown, or wait until the cat wakes up. Come on, Meurig, don't get so down. I've never met such a man for gloom. We've got the candle and now we just have to get out. There must be another tunnel.'

He looked at her in affectionate astonishment. 'Don't you ever give up?'

'No. I won't.' She flung her arms wide. 'I know there's another way out. There's got to be.'

Conor didn't see why, but she had cheered him up and he felt more hopeful. You could always depend on Sara. But Meurig seemed lost in one of his bitter moods.

'What sort of watchman am I?' he snapped. 'All I thought about was the candle . . . I should never have let you make Hafren that promise. Imagine her anger . . . imagine what she'll do . . .'

'The sluices are shut and they'll stay shut and that's what's important,' Sara said firmly. 'Now come on. My feet are getting wet.'

She grabbed him and pulled him up. Already the water had risen further; looking up at the marks on the walls Conor thought that it had much higher to go – certainly higher than his head.

Meurig slung the fiddle over his shoulder. 'All right Sara, let's look. But I don't think we'll find anything.'

They followed her, keeping as far from the sleeping cat as possible. They explored the rippling green darkness, climbing past pools up to the highest curtain of hanging stalactites. Here the ground became drier; there were fewer pools and the light, as if it somehow glimmered from the water, was dimmer.

The ways they tried ended only in rockwalls or piles of rubble, until one passageway looked promising, receding into blackness.

Sara climbed up. 'There's a gap here . . . big enough to get through. It might go somewhere.'

Meurig pulled out the box of matches and tossed it up to her.

'There's only three,' she said doubtfully.

'Just use one then.'

After a moment a sharp blue crack came from her fingers, then a yellow glow; she held up the match and the flame settled, throwing her dim enormous shadow over the wall. They saw her bend into the crack.

'It's big . . . it goes on a long way.'

The flame went out suddenly and they heard her turn. 'It blew out! There's a draught!'

Meurig climbed up quickly. 'You're a wonder Sara, no mistake. I'll go first this time – if I can fit we all can.'

He slung the fiddle tight and edged in, sideways.

Sara stared after him. 'How is it?'

'Dark.' His hand came out for the box and another match spluttered. Light flared, shielded by his hand. 'It goes up,' his voice said, sounding distant. He shuffled on for a few steps, until the match went out.

'Come on,' Sara said, and climbed in.

Conor came last. He felt warmer now, though the scratch on his neck was still sore.

Inside the rocks the tunnel felt surprisingly smooth underfoot. There was certainly a breeze coming from somewhere; he could feel it on his lips and eyes.

Sara paused. 'What's that noise?' They listened to it for a moment; a dull, distant roar, and nearer, somewhere ahead, a soft swish. Odd hollow knocks came from somewhere beneath them. It reminded Conor of the sounds in the watchtower; he wasn't surprised when Meurig answered, 'Water. The sea is all around the island remember, and far under our feet too. We're deep inside it. We'll have to feel the way now – there's only one match and we'd better keep it.'

They moved forward, into blackness. Conor could not feel the sides of the tunnel, or the roof, even when he stretched up.

'It's big.'

'Good.' Sara laughed. 'Better than the way in. We . . .'

A sudden, enormous crash silenced her. The tunnel seemed to move; there was a slither of rocks, a cry, dust. Conor flung himself down instinctively; for a moment he thought the roof was coming in, but nothing fell on his taut back, though the taste of dust in his mouth made him cough.

'Sara!'

'I'm all right! What happened?'

'I don't know. Meurig? Are you all right?'

There was no answer.

'Meurig?' Sara breathed.

A rattle of stones ahead, a long fall, the plip of them in deep water. Then nothing.

14

'He's hurt.'

Conor jerked forward but Sara grabbed at him. 'Be careful! Hands and knees.'

They crawled into the dark, through dust, feeling stones and shards roll under their palms. Almost at once Sara stopped him. 'Feel it?'

'What?'

She took his hand and slid it forward over the ground. 'That.'

He felt an edge, broken and crumbling, and beyond it, nothing. It was a hole, and a big one, sprawling right across the path. Sara leaned over into the dark. 'Meurig?'

There was a movement below, a clatter of stones. Then to their intense relief, his voice. 'Keep back Sara. The edge isn't safe. It gave way under me.'

'Are you hurt?'

'Sore. I've knocked my head . . . I'm a bit dizzy. And I've taken the skin off my hands, or it feels like that.' The voice paused. 'This slope – if I move I'll slither deeper.'

'You don't sound so far down.' Conor wriggled out. 'Hold my waist, Sara, tight.'

He put his palms down the inside of the hole and stretched downwards. Then he squirmed out a bit further, until his chest was well out into nothingness. A few pieces of stone and soil fell; he heard Meurig slip and gasp.

Still they could not touch.

'I'll try going a bit further.'

'For heaven's sake be careful,' Sara muttered, her hands gripping his belt. 'If you fall in you'll pull me over, and then we'll all be finished.'

No sooner had she said it than he almost overbalanced; his hands waved wildly in mid air, and he yelled in alarm. She hauled him back almost at once, but not before his fingers had touched something warm and alive.

'I felt his hand! Down a bit, Sara, just a bit . . . that's it.' He felt the fiddler's firm grip close on his. 'Got him! All right, pull!'

He began to struggle back, Sara dragging at him. It took them five minutes of pulling, with Meurig scrambling and clawing in the darkness, until Conor's back and shoulders were an agony of stretched and aching muscles. Finally he managed to grab the fiddler's coat, and with one last effort Meurig crawled over the lip of the pit and collapsed, breathless and aching, next to Conor. They lay there, uncaring, while the echoes settled.

After a long silence, Conor sat up. 'I feel as though I've been on the rack. I'm at least two inches taller!' In the dimness he saw Meurig move his fingers gently over the fiddle. One string hummed, a soft comforting sound in the dark.

'Is it all right?' Sara said.

'I think so. Luckily it was on my back and I fell

forward.' He still seemed shaken, and in some pain, Conor thought.

'Nothing broken?'

'No, just bruises.'

Reluctantly Sara said, 'Meurig, we should get on . . .'

'I know.' He stood up, unsteadily, and moved one foot carefully forward. A rattle of stones slid into distant water. They passed the hole by feeling the edge but after only a few steps they came to another, gaping treacherously in the floor. Only Sara's outstretched foot saved another fall.

Beyond that were more. At the fourth she stopped and sighed. 'Oh look, this is impossible. It will take hours, if we have to feel like this! And if we hurry we'll be down one of these deathtraps for good.'

In the silence they listened to the sound of water far below, swishing and washing in slow rhythms, filling all the drowned hollows of the island.

Then Meurig moved. They heard the crack of a match, then saw his face clearly for a moment, with a new long scratch down his forehead, lit by a small flame that slowly steadied and grew. All at once Conor could see Sara, her astonished stare, her clenched fists.

'You can't!' she gasped. 'Meurig, you can't do that.'

The fiddler gripped the candle, blood from his hands smeared red on the wax. 'No choice Sara.' He scrambled up. 'We've got to get out . . .'

The flame crackled. They stared at it in horror.

'It's too much,' Conor said.

Meurig looked down at them, his face sharp and edged with candlelight. 'Look Conor, it's me Hafren is angry with, and I have to be there when she comes.

I have to. It's all my fault, my carelessness, my despair. If this is what it costs then so be it.'

'Oh put it OUT,' Sara moaned.

'No.'

'Conor tell him!'

'I have,' Conor said unhappily. 'But it's the only way to get out. He's right.' And yet he knew how much this must be costing Meurig, and he was horrified. The fiddler's hands shook. The candle flickered.

'Hurry up then,' Meurig turned abruptly. 'Life's short enough as it is.'

With the tiny flame to guide them the dangers were obvious. Great chasms and gaps broke open across the path; holes plunged to deep pools of phosphorescent water far below, sometimes stinking with greasy black weed. Most were steeper than the one Meurig had fallen into; he had been lucky. They had to jump several, and without the faint glimmer of the candle flame they would surely have fallen.

When the tunnel widened they saw more clearly the holes that pitted it; they threaded their way between them, over narrow bridges of rock, around brims and edges. They hurried more than was safe, nervous, out of breath. In the dark the candle burned steadily, with the soft hiss of melting wax. Its light flickered up wildly over the walls; threw huge leaping shadows. Their eyes strayed to it, furtively, fearfully.

The passage led up now. They pulled each other wearily over rock falls. The air seemed to grow lighter; looking up, Conor saw far above him a ghostly gleam of daylight, at the top of a narrow chimney.

The three of them paused to stare up at it.

'What do you think?' Meurig muttered.

'Too high.' Conor looked at the tunnel that ran on into blackness. 'We'd never climb up.'

He was right, but they went on reluctantly. That glimpse of distant, unreachable sky brought back all the worry about what Hafren might be doing, far off in the estuary. Meurig gripped the dwindling stub of candle tighter, as if he could somehow make it last.

Then Sara stopped. 'Listen!'

For a long second all they heard was the splutter of the flame. Then, far back, a tiny whisper of sound; the rattle of falling stones.

Conor looked at Meurig. 'The cat!'

'Only too likely.' Meurig walked on, quickly. 'If the water reached it then it would wake up.' He began to run, sending the flame jerking over the low roof. 'Hurry. We must be near the end.'

They ran upwards, aching, their hands and feet sore from crawling and scrambling over rock. The air grew lighter; Meurig pinched out the candle flame with a whisper of relief and jammed the stub deep in his pocket.

'How much is left?' Conor gasped.

'Enough. Look, up there!'

Unbelievably, wonderfully, the tunnel was opening. It spread to a wide track, a bank of millions of tiny shells that crunched and slithered underfoot, and then as they climbed up Conor saw the sky, blue and clear, and smelt the fresh, unmistakeable tang of salt and weed and rock pools. Gulls screamed overhead, and a yell of delight rose in his throat, but as he turned he saw far down the tunnel a lithe white glimmer racing towards them.

'Run!' he yelled.

And they ran, really ran, scrambling and falling down the bank of shingle, spilling out onto a wide beach paved with flat slabs of green rock, crusted with barnacles. Deep pools of sky opened under their feet.

Meurig glanced around. The beach was backed by cliffs, high, sheer, white with gull nests. There was no way up.

'Down to the water!'

They raced to the edge of the rocks. The sea spread a wide frill of white lace over the sodden sand; their feet cut sharp prints that filled and softened.

'Now what?' Sara stared out to sea.

'The ferryman. He said he would wait.'

'It wasn't here he left us.'

'I have the distinct feeling that doesn't matter.'

'Well he'd better be very quick then,' Conor said, glancing back.

The cat sat in the cave mouth. It licked one paw, then slid smoothly upright and paced towards them, through the barnacles and bladderwrack. Above, the birds screamed and soared.

'It won't come into the water, will it?' Conor muttered.

No one answered. Instead they all backed into the sea, feeling its cold soak their boots, drench their feet.

As the cat came on they went deeper; knee-high, swaying as the waves tugged at them, as the rough sand was scoured out from under them.

Snarling, ears flat, the cat reached the water's edge.

'What about swimming?' Sara said.

'It would surely get one of us,' Meurig staggered as a wave slapped him, 'and where would we swim?' He pulled a wry face. 'I'd like to thank you both for your help.'

'We're not going anywhere,' Sara said. 'I hope you're not losing heart again.'

'How can I, with you?'

Conor looked at them both through the spray. 'You're idiots, the pair of you,' he said.

The cat crouched, choosing. Then it stared beyond them, out to sea. Its eyes narrowed. It yowled with rage.

Meurig turned; then with a cry he twisted and dived, and even as his head came up above the water, mist was around him, a faint grey glistening, and in it Conor saw the boat, and the ferryman's silent, huddled form. He pushed Sara towards it, and with a great yell, turned and splashed water furiously at the prowling cat. The cat mewed, its eyes narrowed in the foam and spray. It jumped back, and Conor felt someone grab his arms from behind and haul him up, and even as he fell into the bottom of the boat he saw the cat dissolve; become nothing but a floating patch of foam and bubbles on the incoming tide.

'Where is it?' he gasped. 'Did it drown?'

Sara dragged the soaked hair from her face and looked back at the beach. 'It's gone, that's all. Just gone.' She looked at him and grinned. 'I have to say I thought we'd had it then.'

He picked himself up. 'So did I.' Then he turned and saw the ferryman pulling the oars close beside him, and moved quickly next to Sara, lurching the frail boat.

Silent, drained of all speech, and cold despite the

sun, they let the ghost-craft carry them away from Hafren's island. It dwindled, slowly, a green glint in the sparkling waves.

Conor took his eyes from it at last and looked at the others, seeing how worn and dirty they looked; how the blood had crusted on his own collar and on Meurig's hands, how Sara had a great smudge of dirt down her face. He told her about it and she wiped it off with her sleeve, irritably. 'I'm filthy all over, Conor, but I don't suppose anyone will notice out here, do you?'

The ferryman watched her, his eyes wan.

Conor turned to Meurig. 'Well we made it!'

The fiddler opened his eyes and smiled. 'We were lucky.'

'How's the fiddle?'

'The bag's waterproof.'

'And the candle?'

Meurig opened his hand. The candle, rather smaller, rolled as the boat swayed. He clutched it tight.

'Good.' Conor leaned back. The sun was warming him now, and he felt no seasickness; he was cheerful and relieved. 'We've done all right, haven't we? Considering.'

No one answered him.

'Well?'

'Conor,' Meurig said.

He sat up, took one look at the fiddler's white face and whirled round to stare back at the island.

Swollen, enormous, the cat was pacing towards them over the waves. It had become a creature of mist, its eyes shining, its huge tail thrashing across the sky, leaving drifts of cloud behind it.

Conor clutched his knees and said nothing. None of them could.

Closer, looming high above them now, the cat filled the sky, its eyes narrow, satisfied slits. It raised one paw of mist, bigger than the boat, and slowly, firmly, brought it down on them.

15

Sara screamed; Conor ducked.

But the paw passed right through them and swept up again, its claws dripping.

Furious, the cat struck again, slashing sideways with a swipe that made the air hum, and then again, angrily, bringing a strange cold tingling through Conor's body. The boat swayed as he grabbed the side.

'Keep still,' Meurig snapped. 'It's all right! It doesn't look as though it can hurt us.'

The cat bent closer; they could see its fury. Its great face snuffled against them, as if it would pick the boat up in its mouth like a dead mouse, and shake it, spilling them all out, but even as it tried it found it could not bite a ghost, and they saw its anger change to fear, almost bewilderment.

'Poor old puss,' Sara laughed. 'It's all a bit hard to grasp!'

She giggled as the great tongue of mist rasped over her; Conor saw the enormous teeth, the furry muzzle with its whiskers thick as cables, and reached up to touch it, but his hand too, passed through, and he felt only damp and cold.

'It's there, but it's not there. Or is it us? Are we the ghosts?'

Meurig glanced at the ferryman. 'Perhaps we are.'

Chilled, Conor looked up at the cat. It stood still now, watching the boat slide away. The edges of its ears and fur seemed blurred, fainter.

'It's fading,' Sara said, kneeling up. 'Can you see?'

'It's come too far from the island.' Meurig rubbed his face with the back of his hand and allowed himself a smile. 'I should think its power stems from there. It must wane the further it goes.'

Frailer now, the sky showing through it, the cat watched them go. In a few moments it was almost transparent, its shape loosening and drifting, until Conor found he was looking only at cloud; a long thin mass of it, gently dissolving until the sky was clear.

'Well!' Sara settled back, comfortable in the long rise and fall of the boat. 'Maybe we have got away with it . . . or am I speaking too soon?'

Because the ferryman had paused in his rowing; the boat dipped in a sudden trough. He turned his head and looked back, and at the same time Conor felt a breeze spring up, ruffling his hair and collar.

'What is it?' he said uneasily.

The ferryman turned, and began to row again.

'Can you tell us?' Meurig said.

The ghost-face lifted. When it spoke the voice was strained, and painful. 'She knows, watchman.'

Fearfully, they looked at him.

'The weather?'

'She is coming after you. I feel the anger in the river, the deep swelling, the swift currents. She seeks what you have there, what you have stolen.'

'Stolen!' Meurig said hotly 'How many times do I have to hear that? I've stolen nothing. Nothing!'

111

He bit his lip and was silent. Conor looked at Sara.

The breeze gathered, quickly; their coats flapped. Far off to the west a low, ominous bank of red cloud was rising, dulling the clear sky. The sea became grey and choppy. The frail oars sliced through it, bringing up bubbles and foam and showing the strange sinuous shapes of fish with spiny backs and gaping mouths that swam in agitated shoals deep in the murk.

Conor felt cold again. The boat seemed frailer; mist began to drift from it. He knew they were coming back to their own place at last, back to the estuary swollen with the great tide. The sky grew darker. The boat sank into troughs, plummeting with sudden speed, rising and spinning. Rain splattered on him, and he bent his head, gripping the sides of the boat.

'Will we make it?'

'No,' Meurig whispered.

As he spoke, the squall struck. Hail pelted the boat, turning it white with a stinging hiss, robbing them all of breath. A wave picked the boat up and dashed it forward at tremendous speed, leaving them all in a tangled heap in the bottom, all except the ferryman, who rowed on, untroubled. A green wave rose against them; Conor could see far into it, brown weed floating in the heart of it; then it broke to a white roar, swamping the boat and rushing through the old man's body in a crash of foam. Conor struggled up; he put his hand down and the soft timbers split under his weight; water sloshed into the pockets of his coat.

'We're sinking!'

'Don't be daft,' Sara spat over the side. 'How can you sink a ghost?'

'We can still drown!' He looked at the ferryman. 'Can't we?'

The old man nodded. 'As I did, when she dragged me down, far into the mud and places of pain.' Through the rain and the crash of spray he smiled. 'But she could not hold me. I have escaped her.'

'Then help us to.' Meurig pulled Conor up.

The mist thickened, darkness grew. Conor became aware, through the storm, of a new sound ahead of them, the thrash and slap of waves on a beach, or on the wall, the hiss and drag of shingle.

'Listen!'

'I hear it.' The fiddler caught Sara's arm. 'Are you ready?'

She tried to answer but spray drenched them all. They saw her close her lips tight and nod.

'Guard the wall,' the old man said, unexpectedly. 'Or tonight there will be more drowned faces in her pools.' He gave one last tug on the oars, and the boat pierced the green wall of a wave and slid noiselessly into the narrow pill; the land looming so suddenly out of the dark that Conor was bewildered; he had thought they were still far out in the estuary.

Sara jumped out at once, sinking well into the mud. 'Conor!'

He scrambled over the side, his hands feeling the boat's timbers become faint and cold. Water splashed to his knees; a wave roared in and soaked him, lifting the dissolving ghost of the boat. Meurig was out straight after him; together they squelched through mud and stones to the firmer shingle. When they looked back the ferryman and his boat were nowhere. The estuary churned; wide and empty; the gale drove the tide hard on the land.

Meurig pushed him on. 'Over the wall. We won't be safe until we are.'

They turned, but as Conor put his hand down he felt the vibration under his feet, the huge swelling weight crashing down on him. He scrambled up but the wave knocked him down, drenched him, left him choking in salt and mud and spume. He clung tight to the wall, not breathing. There was a long moment of green; brown weed against his face; pain. Then his head burst out into the air; he snatched a breath and gripped tighter. The wave tore at him as it went back, tore his hair and coat with what he felt sure were hands, Hafren's fingers dragging him. For a moment he thought she had him; then with a wrench he was free, water streaming from his clothes. He scrambled up, leapt the rocks and was over the top of the wall before the next wave could catch him.

It was dark here; spray filled the air. He looked for the others and saw Sara, her face splashed with mud, and Meurig sliding down the bank. They coughed and spat in shocked silence; the waves clawing the wall at their backs.

'Let's get further in,' Conor gasped at last.

Painfully they loped up the track, shivering with cold. When they reached the gate they dragged it shut behind them and crumpled in an exhausted row against the comfortingly solid wood.

Conor wiped his face with his sleeve. He was tired and achingly hungry. He realized they had been gone since morning, with nothing to eat or drink.

'What's the time?'

Sara shrugged, 'My watch is full of water. About seven? It's dark enough.'

Over the hedge a cow coughed, making them jump.

'So we made it. I never thought we would,' Conor said, grinning.

Meurig, beside him, took out the candle from his pocket and held it, a small white glimmer on his palm.

'Now what?' Conor said, looking at it.

'Home. As soon as we can.'

16

The Sea Wall Inn was ablaze with light. The waves battering the wall threw spray high above it; it clattered on the roof like white rain.

Conor tripped over a sandbag and almost fell into the bar. His mother ran out from the kitchen, wet hair plastered to her forehead.

'Oh thank God!' she said. 'Where on earth have you been? Look at the state of you!'

'Nowhere on earth, exactly.' Conor sat down at a table. He felt incredibly tired; his hand throbbed fiercely.

'I was so worried when we came back and you weren't here.' His mother wiped hair from her eyes. 'We've had to leave the van up the lane at Morris's. The road is full of water.' She threw a shocked look at Meurig and Sara, who were crouching over the fire, shivering, and became instantly brisk.

'Right. Dry clothes, hot food. Upstairs Conor, now. Sara, go into my room, you might find a few things you can wear. Meurig . . .'

'I'm quite all right Jill.' The fiddler lay back wearily in a chair, his feet stretched out to the spitting blaze.

'Nonsense. You're soaked. You'll catch your death.'

He smiled. 'On the contrary, I couldn't be better. But I am a bit thirsty.'

Evan came in, his arms round a great sack of sand. He flung it down on the doorstep with a groan, slammed the door and turned to see her handing Meurig a glass of beer. The fiddler drank and sighed. 'Wonderful.'

As Conor pushed Sara upstairs he caught Evan's sour look in the mirror and laughed.

'What's tickling you?' Sara asked.

'Nothing.'

But when she had changed into an old purple jumper and jeans, and was sitting on the floor lacing her shoes he said, 'She likes Meurig.'

Surprised, Sara looked up. 'Well, well. I thought you didn't want her to like anyone.'

'Don't be daft. I don't want her to marry Evan, that's all.'

She laughed. 'You're mad Conor. You've no idea. She doesn't want to marry Evan. Your neck's bleeding again – and she'd tell you if you asked her.'

'How do you know I haven't?'

'Oh I know. I know you.'

Spray rattled the window. Annoyed, Conor jammed on a spare pair of socks and went to look out. A dustbin lid went clanging somewhere down the lane; the gale struck the house with gusts that rattled every door. Beyond the wall the tide was rising fast; even now, with two hours to the top of the tide, the sound of the crashing waves was louder than he had ever remembered it before.

'You're not going home, are you?'

'In this?' She scrambled up. 'I just phoned, anyway. They're all out filling sandbags; Nan says the place is like a fortress. The police wanted them to evacuate but Dad won't leave the stock. She told me to stay put.'

'But it's nearer the wall here.'

She shrugged. 'The wall's never broken yet.'

He went to the door. 'No one's ever robbed Hafren before. I've never heard waves like that.'

Downstairs they ate quickly and in silence, around a table pulled close to the fire, Meurig with his hands washed and carefully bandaged. Evan banged in and out noisily, humping sandbags, carrying things upstairs, treading heavily on the floorboards. Sara grinned at Conor and he shrugged.

'Hot tea.' His mother put down some striped mugs and looked at them all curiously. 'You still haven't told me where you were today.'

They exchanged furtive glances. 'Exploring,' Meurig said, cutting a potato absently into four pieces. 'Wet, dark, horrible places.'

'I can see that. You're a bigger kid than they are!'

He smiled.

'How was the cinema?' Conor asked quickly.

'Oh fine.' She collected the plates. 'I missed you though. Evan rustled toffee papers in the quiet bits. I think he got bored.'

'He would.'

Evan, as if he had heard, came through, and gave them all an irritated glance, especially Meurig. 'You won't get an audience tonight.'

'Never mind.' The fiddler looked ruefully at the damp bag on the floor. 'I don't think I'd be worth hearing.'

A crash of spray against the windows made them all jump. It hissed down the chimney. Conor's mother slammed the windows and bolted them.

'Look, the alert's gone to double red,' Evan said, rubbing his nose. 'Don't you think . . .'

'What?'

'Well, it might not be safe to stay here. The police said . . .'

Jill faced him, angrily. 'This is my house and I'm not leaving it. Not for some village hall in Magor. We've had floods before, if it comes to that.'

'It was just a thought, Jill.'

'Well if you want to go . . .'

'Oh Lord no. Of course I don't.' He nodded, reasonably. 'I understand how you feel. I'll finishing moving the things upstairs.'

'Thanks Evan.'

Thoughtfully, Conor helped Meurig take the dishes out to the kitchen.

'Are you staying?'

Meurig shook his head. 'I'm going to the watchtower. I need to see how things are. I'll be back though.'

Listening to the roar of the waves Conor said, 'It'll be dangerous. Don't think you're safe just because you've got the candle.'

'I know. But I need to see the wall, how it's holding. I'm the watchman . . . it's about time I watched. Like I said, I've thought too much about myself.' He took something from his pocket. It was the candle. He looked at it. Then, deliberately, he held it out. 'I want you to keep it for me. I daren't take it out there.'

Appalled, Conor took it, silently, and put it into his

pocket. The small stub felt cool and slightly clammy. 'Don't be long,' he said, lamely.

Meurig buttoned up his coat. 'Believe me, I won't.' Then he opened the door and slid out into the storm.

When he was gone they worked quickly. The rest of the sandbags were dragged and hauled and flung against doors and windows; shutters were nailed tight; valuables carried upstairs. Outside the gale roared; with still an hour to go the windows were awash with spray. Beyond hearing, like a pounding deep in his head, Conor felt the relentless throb of Hafren's anger, never pausing, never giving in.

At half past ten a crash on the back door made them all turn. Someone banged on it again, hard, and Conor ran to it, thinking it was Meurig, but when the bolts were shot back Mr Caristan stumbled in, rain streaming from his new yellow waterproofs. A small avalanche of mud and water streamed in with him.

'I'm so sorry,' he muttered, fumbling with the zip of his coat. 'Look at the mess!'

Jill smiled bleakly. 'There'll be plenty more later on, don't worry. Another orphan of the storm?'

Sheepishly, he unzipped his coat. 'I'm afraid so. Despite all the warnings I didn't really get enough sandbags . . . it's foolish, I know. I moved all my china to the loft. I was, just, well . . . I couldn't stand it, sitting there, you know, all alone in the house.' He rubbed his hair. 'It was as if I could hear voices. Voices in the wind, screaming . . . fanciful, isn't it? And water began to seep under the door into the hall – as you know the house is in a bit of a hollow. In short, I got scared.' He laughed, nervously. 'I just wanted a few friendly faces. Drown in company, you know. Do you mind, Jill?'

Conor grinned at Sara. His mother shook her head. 'You're a real hero,' she said, not unkindly. 'Well there's plenty of room here. Come by the fire before the rain puts it out.'

'I know I'm a nuisance,' he muttered.

'How's the track out there?' Evan asked.

'Oh knee-deep, I'm afraid, and in some places higher. And the waves! I could hardly get along against the spray, even right under the wall. They must be tremendous.'

'No way out then, even if we wanted to.'

'We don't want to,' Conor growled.

Half an hour passed, slowly. When everything was done they sat in the bar, listening to the fury of the storm, watching the flames hiss and sink under the constant soaking spray that sloshed down the chimney. Finally, they went out. Conor fingered the candle, wondering about Meurig. If he had been swept away they wouldn't even know.

Water had been seeping through the sandbags and under the door for an hour or more; now it lay over the flagstones, trickling down the step into the kitchen. An enormous thump outside made Evan slide the shutter nervously aside.

'Shed's blown down.'

Mrs Jones shrugged, her feet on a chair. 'That happens in most winds.' She dragged the hair from her cheek and winked at Sara. 'The men are nervous. I think we'd better move upstairs.'

As they climbed up Conor muttered. 'I wish Meurig would hurry.'

'He'll be all right,' Sara said.

They went into his bedroom and put the light on, but almost immediately it crackled and sparked and flicked off. None of the switches would work.

'Blast!' Evan snapped. 'Now what?'

'Candles.' Conor's mother came in with three, already lit; their flames threw enormous shadows, making the room alien and unfamiliar. Conor sat on the bed, watching Evan try the radio. 'That won't work. It never does in a storm. Interference.'

'There must be some way we can find out what's going on!' Evan said desperately. 'What are the coastguard doing? What's the storm warning? We're just marooned here.'

'We've no choice,' Conor said briskly. He was enjoying himself now; the big man was nervous, and he knew it.

Evan paced heavily, creaking the floorboards. Mr Caristan sat uncomfortably on the end of the bed.

'Oh sit down Evan,' Conor's mother snapped.

'I just wish we could *do* something.'

'I'll bet Meurig's doing something,' Conor said maliciously.

Sara pursed her lips at him, and he turned and opened the shutter a crack. 'Just look at it out there!'

The night was a roaring blackness. Water blurred the glass; it was impossible to see anything, but they could feel the building shiver and crack around them, the noise of the wind rising to a shriek above the banging and clatter of objects down in the yard. Then Conor caught a movement below and whirled round. 'It's Meurig! Quick!'

He and Sara hurtled down the dark stairs. To his astonishment the kitchen was already knee-deep in water; it rose against his Wellingtons and an empty cardboard egg box bumped his leg as he dragged back the bolts of the door. Meurig slid in, a torrent of water with him. He was drenched, and they knew by his look things were serious. He pushed past them to Conor's mother.

'You'll have to leave.'

'No . . . I can't.'

Meurig took her hands. 'Listen Jill, the wall may be breached, there's a real danger. If it is, this house will be flattened; the sea will surge in and batter it to pieces, you know that. You're too close and way below sea level. Come to the watchtower. It's the safest place. This is what it was built for.'

Unhappily she looked at Conor, then briefly round the kitchen.

'We'd be swept away out there,' Evan said. 'It's madness.'

Meurig ignored him. He waited, until she looked up at him.

'We'll come,' she said.

A shutter crashed; rain splattered their faces. Outside, the wind screamed, like a jealous girl.

17

Conor's coat was still soaked; he pulled it on hurriedly and shoved two packets of crisps from a box into his pocket. Meurig waited by the door; when they were all ready he said, 'Keep together. Keep hold of each other. Once we get in the lee of the wall the wind is less powerful, but the spray is crashing like hail; it's hard to breathe, let alone see.'

'Yes all right,' Evan said impatiently. 'I think we know that.'

Meurig gave him an amused look. 'Right. Go last then, will you?'

For a moment Evan looked as if he would argue; then he shrugged and pulled on his hood.

Meurig unbolted the door. 'Ready? Here goes.' With a sudden jerk he pulled it wide. Water roared in over their knees. 'Dear God,' Mr Caristan whispered.

Staggering, half blind, they waded out, climbing over the sandbags. Evan struggled to shut the door, but the force of the water was too great; he left it and grabbed Caristan's arm.

'It won't shut!'

'Leave it!' Jill pushed Sara on. 'Leave it!'

Meurig had been right. The wind was a wild, battering pain; it slammed them across the car park hard against the fence, and they had to grip the wooden posts and drag themselves along. In the open track it was worse; crossing to the wall Conor fell twice and had to be hauled up, dripping, from the water. He reached shelter with all the breath knocked out of him, soaked again.

Meurig glanced along the line, hair in his eyes. 'All still here?'

Sara laughed, leaning back against the wet slope of the wall. 'This is crazy! Look at the spray!'

Above them the sky was white; sea water fell like hail, drenching them all. Conor felt the wall vibrate, terrifyingly close.

'It's shaking! It moved!'

Wet soil slid under his fingers; fragments of soil slid and trickled. 'Meurig!'

The fiddler was there, his face a mask of rain. 'And up there,' he yelled.

The top of the wall showed a tiny cleft, with a trickle of tide pouring from it. It was small, but they knew it would grow, that Hafren would work it with her wet fingers, dragging down the soil, washing out the roots of the grass, undermining the stones till they slipped and settled and the flood burst through.

'What can we do?'

He saw Meurig shout something.

'What?'

A gust of wind knocked the fiddler against the wall. He picked himself up and hung onto Conor 'Sandbags,' he yelled in Conor's ear.

'Plenty at the pub! But what about . . .'

Conor flung a glance at his mother. If they took bags from the pub the damage would be worse.

'It doesn't matter!' she yelled. 'If the wall breaks there won't be a pub! I'm coming back with you.'

'You're not! Evan will come. Get these youngsters to the tower, please Jill!'

After a second she nodded, and grabbed Conor's arm. 'Let's go.'

They ran, splashing through the mud and seeping floodwater. Halfway down Sara said, 'Where's Caristan?'

Conor looked back. A figure in oilskins waved them on.

'He's coming.'

The watchtower was almost invisible in the storm, all but the windows, high up. Meurig must have left the oil lamp lit, for it glowed up there, a pale square of hope. And the waves leapt up at it, great crashes of spume, slithering down the sheer walls in long sheets of bubbles and foam, and Conor thought, as he ran towards it, that for a moment they were hands, not small, as from the reen, but huge; long, white-nailed fingers tearing at the tower.

Then they were through the spray, and fitting the key in the lock.

Inside, they climbed the steps out of the water and sat slowly, taking breath.

'I can't feel my ears,' Sara moaned.

'I can.' Conor rubbed them. 'I wish I couldn't. We've got to get that door closed.'

He splashed across, and the figure in yellow oilskins slid in and helped him. Together they forced it shut and slid the bolt, feeling the swollen wood strain and crack.

Then the man took his hood off, and they saw it was Evan.

Astonished Conor said 'I thought you'd gone to help Meurig?'

'Caristan went.'

Conor was silent. He heard his mother and Sara move behind him. 'Evan?' his mother said, her voice sounding strange in the echoing tower. 'But Caristan's an old man.'

Evan pushed past her, filling the narrow stair. 'He was gone before I could stop him, Jill, so I came on to look after you. It's a tomfool idea, anyway.'

'Not if it saves the wall.' She whirled round, angrily.

He shrugged and climbed up. Conor looked at Sara and raised his eyebrows. He followed his mother up in silence.

Meurig had left the fire burning, and the lamp lit on the table. The room was wonderfully warm and hushed. The sea might tear at them, but the strong walls were stone, and thick.

They sat down for a while, thawing themselves, listening to the storm. Conor sat next to Sara, steam rising from his knees. He put his hand in his pocket and took out the candle, holding it hidden. Such a small, ordinary thing. Feeling the fire warm it, he pushed it back.

At last his mother lifted her head. 'Here they are!' She ran downstairs; after a time they heard voices, echoing footsteps. Evan sat waiting at the table. He unfolded his arms and leaned back in the chair. Conor thought there would be a row, but when Meurig came in he went straight to the fire and said nothing. Mr Caristan gave Evan a sharp look and pressed his lips tight; he took off his waterproof slowly.

Sara got up and helped him. 'Is it done?'

'As well as we could. Wet sand is unbelievably heavy. My back will never be the same. But we've plugged the gap, and it will be slower to widen. The tide is at the full now. It may make all the difference.' He went to the fire and Conor moved aside. 'Thank you Conor. Very kind.'

For a while no one spoke. It was strange, Conor thought, how a group of people could all be thinking the same thing, and yet none of them wanted to say it. But it hung in the air like a bad smell. Evan had been scared.

Meurig and Sara were angry, and Caristan too polite to say anything, but how did his mother feel? What was she thinking? He looked across at her, as she sat on the bed staring at her wellies, her straight hair masking her eyes.

She glanced up, gave him a quick smile, and stood. 'This won't do. Have you got a kettle, Meurig? Let's have some tea.'

When it came the tea was hot and strong, in two chipped mugs that had to be shared. Mr Caristan looked at his and shook his head. 'When I think of all that beautiful china down there . . . Do you think it will survive?'

Meurig shrugged. 'If the wall holds we'll all survive.'

'I'll make you a small present of a few items,' Caristan said. 'A rather sweet Coalport . . .' He stopped, and stammered '. . . that is . . . if you want it.'

Meurig frowned. 'Thank you.'

Conor knew they were thinking of the burglary. He grinned into his mug.

'About that business . . .' Caristan said suddenly.

'It was my fault,' Meurig said shortly, 'but I wasn't trying to steal anything.'

'No . . . no indeed. But no hard feelings, eh?'

Meurig gave him a sharp look. 'No. It's all finished now.'

There was a short silence.

'The tide must have turned by now,' Sara said, at last.

'Yes.' Meurig stared into the fire. 'But the wind is still a gale. She may well have clawed the wall away. The storm would drown the noise.'

'Who's she?' Evan held the mug and sipped from it noisily. It was the first time he had said anything for a while.

Meurig shrugged, easily. 'Did I say she? I meant the river, of course.'

Later, they tried to sleep. Conor's mother curled up on the bed, and the rest made themselves uncomfortable huddles on the wooden floor. With his head on one of Meurig's pullovers Conor lay still, listening to the crackle of the flames, the moan of the wind. The pullover smelled of woodsmoke; it made Conor remember the night he had first seen the fiddler by the reen, and the fingers of water that groped and slid. Now she was tearing at the tower, and he, inside her enormous fingers, was tiny.

The floor under him shuddered as a great wave crashed against the wall; down below him, through the floor he could hear the strange sloshing and knocking and trickle of water in the base of the tower. He closed his eyes and thought of the inn, drowned as in his dream, his clothes floating out of the wardrobe. Then he saw the wall, buckling and weakening, soil sliding from it, the cat's great white paw tearing it down, licking at it with a tongue of foam, licking him too, and biting his arm. He shrugged it off, but it grabbed him again with its soft mouth and shook.

'Wake up,' Sara breathed.

He rolled over and sat up, quickly.

The room was dark; the fire had sunk to a glimmer. The sky outside was slightly pale, as if beyond the clouds the morning was coming. His mother, Evan and Caristan were asleep, dim breathing shapes, but Meurig's blanket was empty.

'He's downstairs.'

'So?'

'He's talking to someone.'

Silent, he stood. They crept between the sleepers, slipped out of the door and closed it softly. The stairwell was damp; the water below slapped and knocked on stone.

'Hear it?' Sara whispered.

Voices drifted from below, quiet and distorted.

Conor went down the dark steps carefully. 'Did you see him go?'

'No. I just heard.'

Lamplight flickered below on the green walls, showing Meurig's long shadow. He turned, quickly, the oil lamp in his hands. 'Who's that?'

'Only us. Who were you talking to?'

'He was talking to me.'

The voice, cold as winter, came from the open doorway. The waves washed in, and she stood waist-deep in them, her dress storm grey, swirling into the tide.

He came closer; Meurig jumped up a step and Conor noticed the lower ones were wet. The tide was ebbing.

'I was wrong.' She stepped closer, in the quavering glints and rippling reflections on the walls. 'I will need to watch you.'

'It's my job to watch you,' Meurig muttered.

She came one step out of the water; it streamed from her dress and sleeves and down the long weed-strewn hair. 'You have your life now. But remember, the spell is on you and can never be put out. You will never be out of my reach. We are bound, watchman, each to each.'

'I know that,' he whispered.

'Your friends,' she hissed, 'must be cleverer than they look.'

'Thanks,' Sara muttered drily.

A wave surged in and splashed right up over Meurig; he leapt up the steps, water running from his pockets.

'Do you think I would have it here? I will put it somewhere where you'll never find it!'

With a shock Conor retreated back up the steps. He had forgotten he had the candle in his pocket! He felt cold.

The creature smiled; a twisted, uncanny look. 'Where is there I cannot come? Bury it, and I will send threads of myself smaller than worms through the soil. I will watch from every reen, puddle and pool. Every drain. And I will not tire, candleman. This wall will wear away under my hands. Year by year I will unpick it with my fingers.' She sank into the water, her hair spreading. 'I have all the time I need. Men die. I will always be here.'

It was true and they knew it. She drifted under the water, the pale oval of her face rippling for a moment under the floating foam. Then a wave washed over her, and she was gone.

18

The mud on the floor of the bar was inches thick; it coated the fallen stools and made a heavy brown stinking layer over the cold ashes of the fire. Jill hauled the shutters open; the bleary, grey light flooded the room.

'Dear God,' she said, 'look at it.'

And yet they all knew they had been lucky. The shutters had held, and apart from a few slates, so had the roof. In a week the mud would be cleared, and apart from a new green flood mark, which Conor would label with the year and the date, they had survived the river's anger. But if there were flood marks on people's hearts, Conor thought, Meurig's at least would be scarred.

But they'd made it. And it would be the same in all the houses and farms on the Levels this morning; clearing up, and being thankful that the wall still loomed over the sodden fields.

Mr Caristan had already gone, hurrying to his precious china. He'd even shaken Meurig's hand and said, 'I meant it, you know, about the Coalport.'

Meurig nodded. 'Thanks, but I'd probably only break it.'

Mr Caristan tried not to look appalled. 'Well, it is meant to be used,' he said bravely. 'And it's thanks to you I've still got it.'

'Thanks to both of us.'

Mr Caristan looked pleased, and shy. 'Maybe, in a little way, I may have helped.'

When he was gone Meurig turned to Jill. 'Look, can I borrow Conor? It won't take long – about an hour.'

She wiped her fingers on a rag, absently. 'If you like. But get him back because there'll be plenty to do here for days. And don't forget you're playing here tonight.'

'We're not opening!' Evan looked at her in surprise.

'We certainly are.' She pulled her boot from the mud. 'It takes more than a foot or two of sea water to keep the Sea Wall closed, I can tell you. Last time we had a flood we could only serve spirits for a week, and that did wonders for trade.' She put an arm round Sara and smiled. 'You should be getting home. They'll be worried.'

'I know. Thanks, Mrs J.'

Evan went into the kitchen, shaking his head. Conor followed Meurig and Sara to the door. 'I won't be long.'

'Fine.'

He lingered for a moment in the room. 'You'll be all right for now?'

His mother looked up at him in surprise. 'Look Conor, I can manage. I do run this pub myself, you know.'

He nodded, drily. 'I know.'

'There you are then.' She came over to him, and

leaned her hand against the doorpost. Then she said, 'Floods don't just wash things away, do they? They leave things behind them as well. And they tell us a lot about our friends, don't you think?'

'I suppose so.'

'Well they do. So don't worry.' She brushed the damp hair from his forehead. 'It's all over, and we're all still here. And I'm the licensee, Conor. I'm in charge. You're a funny old worrier. Don't you know by now I can look out for myself?'

He smiled, and looked down. 'Yes, I know you can,' he said, and he turned and ran out after Meurig and Sara, ran hard down the splashing track, wanting to shout and jump and yell in the blustering wind. He hurtled past Sara and whirled, running backwards, 'Come on! Let's see the damage!'

Racing up the steps, not caring whether they followed, he leapt to the top of the wall and the wind struck him, and he stared out with wet eyes at the great banks of brown, popping mud and far beyond it the distant silver line of the Severn, where flocks of waders formed their glittering, wheeling clouds.

She had gone. She had withdrawn, shrunk to a narrowness far off, and as always he was astonished at the speed and reach of her, how she could drown such a vast expanse of land twice every day, at the power of the moon and the tide.

They walked along to the place where the gap had begun. Meurig crouched and looked at it. The gap had been clogged with bags; below it the soil had seeped slightly, leaving a hole the size of a fist. 'That will have to be repaired properly,' he muttered.

Sara said, 'What happened, with Evan? He said . . .'

'Never mind what he said.' Meurig stood up and

they followed him along the wall. 'He was scared, that's all. Caristan was scared too, but the difference was, he stayed. Makes me sorry I didn't try harder with him in the beginning . . . None of this might ever have happened.' He turned to Conor quickly. 'You've still got it safe?'

Conor put his hand to his pocket but Meurig said, 'Not now. Not here.'

'He's got the candle?' Astonished, Sara leapt down the steps and opened the farm gate. 'You trusted him with that!'

'Apparently.'

'You're mad!' she said firmly. 'I'll bet he even forgot he had it.'

They watched her run up the drive, waving.

'Did you forget?' Meurig asked quietly.

'Of course not.' Conor jammed his hands in his pockets and changed the subject. 'Where are we going, anyway?'

'Newport.'

'Like this!' He knew he was filthy; there were clots of mud in his hair and his clothes were damp and stiff.

Meurig strolled on to the bus stop. 'Who cares?'

On each side of the lane the swollen reens lay green and replete. Pools spread over the track; twigs and drowned worms floated in them. When the bus came they flagged it down and sat at the back, the only passengers. It wandered slowly through the wet lanes, the driver talking all the time over his shoulder about the storm. Spray hissed from the tyres and ran down the windows.

In Newport they got off.

'Where now?' Conor said. He still couldn't see

what Meurig was up to, but it was obvious the fiddler had some plan.

For answer Meurig looked up at the the huge building in front of them, the Royal Bank of Wales, all marble facade and stucco magnificence.

'In there?' Conor said, appalled.

The fiddler nodded. He pushed open the plate glass doors and walked in boldly, across the immense, echoing hall, leaving a trail of mud over the plush, plum-coloured carpet, straight to a window marked Enquiries. Conor trailed reluctantly behind.

The cashier looked up. 'Can I help you?'

Meurig brushed muddy hair from his eyes. 'I've got some property – very valuable property,' he snapped. 'I want to put it in a safety deposit box and keep it here.'

The girl's eyes widened. She flicked a glance at the fiddler's torn, drenched coat, the frayed sleeve of his pullover. 'I see.'

Conor fidgeted. He was sure people were staring. One kid with her mother giggled and pointed. He pulled a sliver of weed off his neck and jammed it in his pocket.

Meurig filled in the forms the girl gave him, quickly and carelessly. At the part where it said 'Nature of Valuables' he wrote 'one candle' in his spiky script, signed it, and pushed it back across the counter.

The girl read it; her eyebrows shot up.

'I'll just check this with the manager, sir.'

'You do that,' Meurig muttered.

They watched her cross the floor to a thin man in a grey suit; there was a hurried conversation. The man stared at them.

'Are you sure you want to do this?' Conor muttered. 'I mean, you wouldn't have it with you . . .'

'I know.' Meurig watched the manager stalk towards him. 'But where could be safer than here? I can't think of anywhere else.'

Down in the vaults, the manager rattled his keys, selected one, and after a dubious look at Conor, lifted out a small metal box with the number 77 painted on it in white. He brought it to the table and opened it. Then he stepped discreetly away.

'Wait!' Meurig said quickly. 'Listen. No one will have access to this, will they? No one at all?'

The man looked hurt. 'I assure you sir, the boxes are never opened by anyone except the owners. You will have the key. Your . . . valuables will be perfectly safe.'

'I hope so,' Meurig said desperately. 'It's just that . . . what I keep in here is very, very precious. It's a matter of life and death.'

The manager looked at Meurig as if he was mad. 'It'll be safe, sir,' he stuttered.

Meurig sighed and nodded to Conor; Conor took the candle out and gave it to him. The fiddler rolled it in his long fingers. 'Well,' he said softly, 'rest here and don't torment me any more.' He put it in, closed the metal box and locked it. Then he turned to the manager, who had been watching curiously. 'All yours.'

As the box was lifted they heard the candle roll inside, a small ominous sound, but Meurig turned firmly and marched through the thick iron doors of the vault and back upstairs.

Out on the street, they sat for a while on the plinth of a statue, looking, Conor thought, like a pair of tramps. He hoped none of the girls from school would come by.

'That's used up all my money,' Meurig said at last.

'I've got enough for the bus.'

'Then let's get back.' The fiddler stood up. 'You've got your mother to help and I've a fiddle needs tuning.'

'Meurig,' Conor said quietly. 'Look. Over there.'

The fiddler turned.

On the opposite pavement, outside the fishmongers, a small white cat sat washing. Its eyes were amber slits. It watched them intently.

'Coincidence,' said Meurig, after a moment.

'It might not be. She'd want to know where it is!'

'Let her.' Meurig turned and walked away. 'We've beaten her, Conor, at least where the candle is concerned. The wall we must guard for ever, but she'll never torment me like that again.'

Conor walked after him. Then he stopped and glanced back. The cat licked a paw and flicked out its claws and washed them, one by one. Then it got up and stalked off, towards the river.